The Pirates Quest Collection

Pirates Quest, Volume 1

Maryse Dawson

Published by Maryse Dawson, 2024.

THE PIRATES QUEST COLLECTION

First edition. July 1, 2024.

ISBN: 979-8231377923

Written by Maryse Dawson.

Table of Contents

TIDES OF DESIRE
THE PIRATES QUEST BOOK I

Chapter One

The English Channel, 1820

The salty breeze whipped through Bess's long, dark tresses as she stood at the helm of her magnificent ship, *the Blue Belle*. Her emerald green eyes scanned the horizon through her spyglass, looking for potential targets. It was the maiden voyage of her newly acquired vessel, and the anticipation of future riches coursed through her veins.

She lowered the spyglass and glanced at her long-time friend, Cat, standing by her side, her arms folded across her ample chest, as she too looked for a ship to loot. Her long blonde hair fluttered slightly in the evening breeze, her keen blue eyes intent on the horizon.

Between them, one dark and one blonde, they were a sight to behold. Their beauty, as well as their prowess, was becoming legendary.

Together, the two women had shared countless adventures. They had become an unstoppable force, cunning and swift, leaving a trail of bewildered victims in their wake.

Bess glanced at the fine lines of their new ship. She was beautiful. Their previous ship had been damaged beyond repair in her last battle, and they reluctantly had to part with the fine galley. But they had chosen to preserve her name. So now, in a way, *the Blue Belle* still sailed on. She laughed to herself. It was amazing how attached one could get to a ship.

As the sun dipped below the horizon, casting a fiery glow across the darkening sky, she nudged her friend gently. "It doesn't look like we're going to find anything tonight, Cat. I think I'll retire for the night, and to be honest, I'm a little weary."

Cat looked at her sideways and said, "I don't suppose it has anything to do with the fact you got rather drunk last night." She laughed.

Bess pursed her lips and said, "I didn't get drunk as such; I was just a little tipsy!"

"You were drunk! That pirate, what was his name? Oh yes, Julio—he was after you and slipped you an extra rum or two. If I hadn't been there, you would have ended up in his bed!"

Bess's expression grew dreamy, remembering the handsome pirate they had met at the small tavern near the beach. "He was rather lovely. Did you see the size of his arms?"

"He was also plying you with drinks! No man should do that or need to do that to get a woman in bed. Handsome he might have been, although that's questionable, but I'm glad I got you back on the ship before anything happened."

Bess grimaced a little. "I suppose you're right."

"You know I am!" She admonished her. "Besides, Lord Fairchild is waiting for you at home, and he wants to marry a virgin."

"So? He would never have known. There are things you can do to fool people." Bess chewed her bottom lip. "Besides, I'm only marrying him because my father wants me to."

Cat threw her a look of exasperation. "I thought you loved him?"

Bess had the grace to look a little shame-faced. "Well, I thought I did. I mean, he's a handsome fellow, but truly, he has such a serious countenance. He never smiles or seems to enjoy anything. As for his conversation, it's almost non-existent."

Cat thought for a moment and then said, "Perhaps that's what married life is about. Being with someone just for the security of their wealth and standing in society? I'm not sure I would want that."

Bess nodded, looking blankly out at sea while thinking of the double life she led. At home, she was Elizabeth Warren, the daughter of a respectable lawyer, and was expected to uphold certain societal expectations, including marrying into money.

She had been betrothed to Lord Clarence Fairchild for nearly six months and had done her best to delay the wedding, but she didn't know how much longer she could postpone the damn thing.

She shuddered a little, thinking of having to sleep with him. She couldn't help but feel that it would be a waste of her life. What if he was as dour in bed as he was out of it?

She immediately pictured the handsome Julio, and her eyes glazed over. Now he would know how to treat a woman; she was sure of it!

But Cat was a true friend and had stopped her from making, perhaps, a silly mistake. As fulfilling and adventurous as it may have been, she thought, sighing wistfully.

Cat's full name was Catherine Penley, and Bess had had the good fortune to meet her five years ago at one of the taverns in Portsmouth, close to her hometown of Somerstown.

They both led quite different lives from each other. Bess was from a large, wealthy estate, whereas Cat had been born out of wedlock and had been given up for adoption as an infant.

Cat had no idea who her real parents were, but it had never mattered. The couple who had adopted her were not only wealthy enough to give her a home but also the love and care a child needs. They already had one son, Connor, who was five years her senior, and Cat had always considered him to be her true brother.

It had been a wonderful childhood, but everything changed when she reached the age of sixteen. Both her adoptive parents had contracted smallpox and, within days, had succumbed to the terrible disease, leaving her and Connor penniless.

Connor was already working as a coxswain on a large ship, but his income wasn't sufficient for both of them. Not until he'd worked his way up the ladder, and that could take years. So she immediately started looking for work herself and found a job at the local tavern, *the Fisherman's Joy*. The owner, Mr Clark, had given her free accommodation on top of her small wage. He was a kindly man, and Cat felt she could never repay him enough.

A few months later, Connor, fed up with working on merchant ships and being paid low wages while being worked like a dog, decided to join *the Blue Belle's* crew, a notorious pirate ship. That way, he'd get a share of any booty, and it had proved extremely worthwhile. Two years later, with the captain injured and having shown a natural ability for leadership, the reins were handed over to him.

He had quickly asked Cat to join him as his first mate. She was feisty and easily capable of working alongside him.

All had been well for the next few years. But a skirmish between his vessel and a British merchant ship of the East India Company, unfortunately, ended in his demise. A shard of wood from the ship's bow had lodged in his brain, and his days on the high seas had come to an abrupt end. Cat had been devastated, but with the crew's support and dedication, they had helped pull her from the pit of despair.

So *the Blue Belle* suddenly had no captain. Cat now had enough experience to command the ship herself, but she was a little nervous, and she wasn't certain the crew would accept a female as their captain.

And that was when Cat met Bess.

Bess had been restless one day, and with time on her hands, she'd left home for a day out seeking excitement and stimulation.

Daring to go into the tavern unaccompanied, she took a seat and ordered a drink. When Cat spotted her sitting alone, she immediately noticed that Bess seemed a little on edge and asked if she could join her. They began talking and warmed to each other right away.

They discovered that they were both the same age, twenty-one at the time, and both possessed not only a need for excitement but also fiery tempers. It was then that Cat told her about her half-brother Connor's recent demise and the life she led out at sea.

Bess was in awe and didn't seem the least perturbed by Cat's outrageous lifestyle. In fact, she seemed quite excited about it.

So Cat took the opportunity to ask Bess if she would join her. Together, they could look out for one another, and Bess would get all the excitement she needed.

It hadn't taken long for Bess to make her decision, and she had taken on a life of piracy as though she were born for it. It had started as a little fun, a way to unleash her frustrations with society and vent her spleen on the high seas, but she soon realised it was much more than that. It was her lifeline to happiness and excitement. Something she lacked at home.

As a ruse, she had told her father that she was staying with an elderly relative in Kent, their great-aunt Hilda. Her father was so busy that he would never have time to visit, and when she returned home, she simply told him a web of lies, and he quite happily believed them!

The Blue Belle had a fine crew, but at first, as Cat had feared, they were a little reluctant to accept a woman as their captain. Some of them mumbled that having one woman on board was bad enough, but two could cause them major problems, rambling on about curses and women being a jinx.

But when Cat and Bess showed them how capable they were, they soon settled down, and now they looked out for one another as a family. In fact, the crew could be a little overprotective on occasion.

"Have you finished daydreaming?" Cat interrupted her thoughts, quickly bringing her back to the present.

"Oh, sorry. I was miles away." Bess answered, smiling.

"You must be tired! Go on. You go to bed. I'll stay on watch until McGregor comes on duty."

McGregor was the quartermaster. A big, burly, red-bearded giant of a man hailing from Scotland. Just one look at him could put the fear of God into anyone they attacked. He was one of their biggest assets.

Bess crossed the main deck and headed to her shared quarters. The captain's cabin was a good size, and with a little rearrangement, they had set up two narrow beds, with comfort being a high requirement.

Closing the door behind her, Bess quickly changed into her nightclothes before collapsing onto the bed. Closing her eyes, she was asleep in minutes.

The next morning, Bess awoke to sunlight filtering through the lattice windows. She stretched and turned on her side, only to see Cat's bed empty. Rubbing her eyes, she sat up and pushed her hair off her face.

She could feel the swell of the sea beneath the ship's bow as she sliced through the waves, and as always, it gave her a sense of excitement.

Throwing the covers aside, she stepped out onto the wooden floor and padded over to the small closet in the corner. With a quick wash and taming her hair into soft waves beneath a bandana, she dressed in black breeches, a white loose blouse, and a burgundy corset.

Just as she finished, Cat walked into the cabin. "Ah, you're up. I left you to sleep a bit, as I think you needed it."

"I feel so refreshed. I can take on anything today!" Bess laughed. "Although not before a satisfying cup of coffee and something to eat."

"Jonas should be bringing us something in a minute. I just popped down to see him." She sat down at the desk and put one of her booted feet on the desk. "Talking of which, I just learned something interesting."

"Oh? Do tell!" Bess said, taking a seat opposite her.

"Jonas said he's heard a rumour that there's a new ship in these parts. When he was last in Portsmouth, he met up with the crew from *the Firefly,* and they spoke about an encounter they had with *the Avalon.*"

Bess frowned. "I've never heard that name before. Who's the captain?"

"Captain Bill." Cat tapped her fingers on the desk. "Apparently, *the Firefly* was en route to intercept a merchant ship, and he simply sailed past them and took it for himself—without so much as a by-your-leave. His ship simply left them standing in his wake."

"The ignorant devil!"

"Indeed. I mean, seriously, how dare he encroach upon their territory?" Cat exclaimed indignantly. "It would seem he's a man with no care for anyone but himself."

"Where is his honour?" Bess demanded, "I know pirates are not known for their generosity to others, but amongst ourselves, surely it's common courtesy to leave the pickings for the first ship that arrives."

"Usually. But not on this occasion. Apparently, he's a very skilled swordsman. The crew of *the Firefly* watched him defeat several men on his own. He stands a head taller than most men and has muscles to match." She pulled a face. "He sounds quite fearsome. I'm not sure I wish to encounter him."

"We have McGregor!" Bess said proudly, "An easy match, if you ask me. Besides, both you and I can handle our swords very well. He'll have a bit of a problem if he dares try to take our rich pickings!"

"If his ship is faster than ours, we won't have much choice."

"He'll rue the day if he dares intercept a ship in our sights!" Bess expressed angrily. "If he takes the booty, then we'll plunder his ship! See how he likes it."

"Those are very brave words, Bess. I just hope we don't encounter the arrogant rogue."

Jonas arrived with a tray of food for them and some freshly brewed coffee. He placed it on the desk, and they both thanked him before diving into the delicious fare.

As *the Blue Belle* sailed onwards, Bess couldn't help but return Cat's sentiments. An encounter with the menacing Captain Bill was something she would rather never happen, and she could only pray that it didn't.

Mid-morning, Bess stood at the bow of the ship, scanning the horizon for her next target. The wind ruffled her hair, and she smiled to herself. It was a good day for a chase. With the wind in their sails, they could catch just about anything!

Cat joined her, spyglass in hand and smiling broadly. "We have the wind in our favour today, Bess."

"I think it won't be long before our coffers are bulging under the weight of treasure, my dear Cat!"

Her words were interrupted by a shout from the crow's nest. "Ship ahoy, Cap'n!"

Immediately, both women raised their spyglasses and scanned the horizon.

"I see it!" Cat said.

"It appears to be a merchant vessel off the port side," Bess said. "She looks like she could be hiding some rich treasures, if you ask me!" Her voice was filled with excitement.

Cat smiled, her blue eyes glinting with mischief, and she called over to McGregor. "Set a course to intercept them, McGregor! It's time we filled our coffers again."

The crew sprang into action at Cat's command, trimming sails and turning the wheel. Soon, *the Blue Belle* was racing across the waves towards their prey. As they drew nearer, Bess studied the merchant ship through her spyglass. All seemed normal until she spotted a second ship breaking through the mist behind their target.

What the hell was going on? She moved her spyglass along the hull until she saw a name that made her blood run cold.

With a snarl, she lowered her spyglass and looked at Cat. "It's *the Avalon*!"

"What?!" Cat cried in alarm.

"I bet he's after our merchant ship!" Bess said grimly, raising the spyglass again. "He's fast. Very fast. Arrogant bastard. But you're not going to get your own way today, Bill, not on our waters!" she muttered angrily under her breath.

Cat urged the crew to move the sails—anything to help them get more speed—while Bess watched and waited to see who would get to the merchant ship first. Pray God it was them.

Chapter Two

Captain Bill stood proudly at the wheel, guiding his beloved ship, *the Avalon*, with expert precision as it cut through the choppy sea. His keen eyes, hidden beneath his black tricorn hat, had spotted his prey—a plump merchant vessel laden with riches.

With a grin, he bellowed commands to his crew. "All hands on deck; we haven't got all day! We've got some treasure to plunder!" The crew scrambled into action, readying the cannons and raising the Jolly Roger. In no time, they had gained on the merchant ship, which appeared to be unaware of the predator stalking it.

He grabbed his spyglass and took another look. "Oh yes, she's a beauty, alright. Like a ripe fruit waiting to be plucked. What treasures lie within your holds, eh?"

He turned to his men. "What say you, lads? Shall we help ourselves?" A roar of approval rose up in response. He knew exactly how to rile his crew up in readiness for an assault. With a devilish smirk, he tapped his cutlass against his boot. "Then the plunder is ours!"

The Avalon drew nearer to the merchant ship, and the tension in the air became palpable. The crew readied their cannons, their fingers itching to light the fuses on Bill's command.

Finally, the time came. Captain Bill raised his cutlass high into the air, signalling the attack. The cannons roared, sending fiery projectiles hurtling towards the merchant ship, tearing through its defences with merciless force.

Bill waited. Would the other ship retaliate? *The Avalon* was a much larger vessel, and if the other captain had any hope of saving his ship, then to capitulate was in his best interest.

As he had hoped, when the smoke cleared, the other captain was standing and glaring at him from the opposite deck.

Bill immediately grabbed a rope, hoisted himself easily onto the railing, and shot the captain a calculated smile. "I take it you will surrender?"

The captain's lip curled back, and he snarled, "Never!"

And with a loud roar, the other crew began to swarm onto the deck. Bill didn't waste any time and shouted loudly. "Attack!"

Grappling hooks were hurled across the divide, and with Bill at the forefront, his cutlass dancing through the air, he led his crew in a ruthless onslaught. The merchant sailors, hopelessly outmatched, did their best to counter the assault but eventually had to give way to Bill's superior force.

Their treasures, once coveted, were soon loaded onto *the Avalon*, much to the delight of Bill and his victorious crew.

Bess watched through her spyglass with growing fury as Captain Bill's crew methodically emptied the hold of the merchant vessel, carrying off its stolen bounty. Her hands gripped the rail of *the Blue Belle* so tightly that her knuckles turned white.

"Arrogant bastard!" she spat.

"He doesn't even care that we're here! It's as though we're invisible." Cat snarled, pacing up and down next to her, her face red with anger.

McGregor was just as het up. "I reckon we should attack him. Teach him a lesson."

Bess lowered her spyglass and looked at him. "I'd like nothing more than to steal back what's rightfully ours, but could we beat him?" She flung her hand out. "Look at the size of his ship! I don't think we'd stand a chance."

She raised the spyglass again and caught sight of him, a broad smile on his face as he spoke to another crew member. His pearly whites shone even from that distance, and for some reason, it made her even more annoyed. "Although, I'd love to wipe that smile off his face!" she said, her eyes narrowing with hatred.

Cat pulled a face and said, "So would I! But if his sword skills are as good as they say, we'd be in for a right bloody battle!"

Bess lowered her spyglass again. "Well, we have to do something. We can't just let him get away with it, can we?" She thought hard. "I think we should at least have a word with him. Let him know that what he did goes against the unspoken rules of piracy."

McGregor raised an eyebrow and said, "Never heard it called that before."

She pursed her lips. "Well, they are rules. What he did was wrong, and we have to tell him so."

Cat nodded in agreement. "You're right. We can't let this happen again." Turning to McGregor, she said, "Set a course straight at him!"

With a quick stride, he took hold of the wheel and began bellowing out orders to the crew. Bess called the first mate over and said, "Jasper, raise the flag and prepare the men for battle. It may not come to it, but just be prepared!"

"Will do!"

With a wicked look on her face, she placed her hand on the hilt of her cutlass and said under her breath, "Well, Bill, let's see what you're made of!"

Bill stood proudly on the deck, his muscular arms folded across his broad chest and grinning from ear to ear whilst looking down into the hold.

Alec, his quartermaster, stood by his side, nodding happily with satisfaction. "What a bounty, eh, Captain?"

"Indeed, it is. I reckon we should sample some of that fine wine tonight, don't you?"

"And the rum! Don't forget the rum!' Alec guffawed.

"I think taking that stash of rum riled the captain more than anything." Bill laughed, remembering the look of rage on the other man's face as he sailed away on his empty ship.

Just then, John Harlen, the first watchman, approached. "Ship approaching, Cap'n. Starboard side."

Bill quickly went into action and strode to the railing. Raising his spyglass, he located the ship. "It's coming straight at us! Ready, crew! Make haste!"

Alec frowned, his experienced eyes quickly spotting the flag. "They're flying the Jolly Roger."

"Pirates? What're they doing coming for us? Damn their eyes!" Bill snapped.

The ship was approaching fast, the wash of the small waves easily visible as the hull cut through the deep-blue sea.

Bill narrowed his eyes. They appeared to be in a hurry. If they thought they were going to get his bounty, then they could think again.

Turning to Alec, he said, "Stand fast and be prepared to board on my command."

Alec instantly joined John as they prepared for battle. Bill waited, his body like a coiled spring, ready for a confrontation.

As the ship neared, he caught sight of a big red-bearded pirate. He looked quite fearsome, but Bill was just as huge. His eyes sparkled with malice. He would be the first to fall if they dared to attack!

The ship turned as it began to draw alongside, and Alec quickly noted the ship's name. "Captain, it's *the Blue Belle*."

"Who's the captain? Do you know?" Bill asked. "Is it old Red Beard?" He eyed the big man, whose countenance was decidedly firm as he locked eyes with him.

Daniel, the second mate, chimed in, "No, Cap'n. I 'eard that they 'ave a female captain!"

"I 'eard it was two!" John added, his eyebrows raised.

Bill's fierce expression changed to one of surprise. "Women captains?"

He didn't have long to wait before *the Blue Belle* drew alongside, and a feisty-looking, dark-haired woman stepped up to the railing. Her eyes sparkled with anger, and placing her hands on her hips, she called over, "Captain Bill, I presume?"

He could tell by her whole countenance that she was extremely vexed, although he wasn't sure why yet. What he did know was that she was one of the finest women he had ever seen.

He bowed and shot her a wide grin. "At your service, my lady. And you are?"

She raised her chin in a show of strength and told him her name. "Captain Bess." And then, her eyes flashing with anger, she said, "Do you know you're trespassing on our territory?"

"Yours? I don't see your name on it."

Another woman edged forward. This one was blonde and equally as pretty. Her lips were tight with anger, and she spat out, "Of course it doesn't have our name on it. But all pirates know these are our waters!"

He regarded her silently, noting her stance and the way her hand remained settled on her cutlass. They were both used to fighting by the looks of things, but as for piracy rules, she was deluded, for there were none.

"Yes," Bess continued, "and you've just stolen what is rightfully ours!"

Bill grinned infuriatingly at her obvious rage. "Well, that's just bad luck," he called across the divide. "Maybe next time you'll be quicker. First come, first served!"

Bess's eyes flashed. "Mark my words, Bill, you'll pay for stealing our prize. No one plunders our waters and gets away with it."

Bill chuckled. "Is that so? Well then, perhaps you'd best come over here and teach me a lesson." With a movement quicker than the human eye, he grabbed a rope and swung neatly across the gap onto the deck of *the Blue Belle*.

Bess drew her cutlass instantly, pointing it warningly at his throat. "You've got a lot of nerve, boarding my ship without permission. Give me one good reason why I shouldn't run you through where you stand."

Red-beard was right behind her, and the blonde woman was at her side. Both with their cutlasses ready to strike.

But Bill only smiled, unperturbed by the blade against his skin. "Now is that any way to treat a fellow pirate? I only came to discuss terms. What say we continue this chat over a bottle of rum, eh?"

He watched Bess's expression, and when he saw the briefest flicker of uncertainty, he acted. Before she had a chance to react, he had disarmed her in a heartbeat and had her trapped against his hard body. His eyes sparkled with malice at red-beard and the other woman.

"Step any closer, and you'll regret it. If you wish your captain to remain unharmed, then you'll step aside."

He felt Bess struggle in his arms, but her strength was no match for his, and she soon gave up.

The other woman went to step forward, and Bess stopped her. "Don't, Cat."

"Cat, is it? That's an unusual name," Bill remarked. "Now, Cat, I'm taking your captain to my ship, where we're going to have a rum and discuss the rules of the high seas. Trust me, she'll not be harmed."

Before anyone could stop him, Bill threw Bess over his shoulder and, with a wicked grin, swiftly swung back to his ship.

Bess struggled furiously as Bill's large hands grasped her arms, but to no avail. With ease, he carried her across the deck, ignoring her pounding fists and curses.

When they reached his cabin, he plopped her unceremoniously onto the bed.

"Now, sweet Bess, there's no need for such a fuss," he chided, dodging the kick she aimed at his head.

"You bastard! How dare you do this?" Bess cried.

But Bill only laughed, his hazel eyes dancing with amusement at her fiery spirit. He hadn't encountered such a feisty woman for a long time and was thoroughly enjoying the interchange.

"I haven't done anything yet!" He exclaimed, walking over to a cabinet. "Now, a rum, I think. Perhaps it will calm you down a bit."

Against her will, Bess felt a tug of attraction—the man was devilishly handsome, to be sure. His wavy, dark hair reached his shoulders, and the sheer size of him was a turn-on. She blinked rapidly, wondering where her thoughts were heading!

Annoyed with herself, she snapped, "You stole our prize, and that's low even for a pirate! We follow codes in these waters."

Bill poured two glasses of rum, offering one to her. "Codes be damned! Out here, it's survival of the fittest. If you can't defend your plunder, you don't deserve to keep it."

Bess gasped at his arrogance, and without thinking, she hurled her glass at him with a snarl, splashing rum across his shirt. The glass fell to the floor and rolled under the desk.

"We'll see about that!" she vowed. "If I see you again in our waters, I won't hesitate to attack you. So be warned!"

She scrambled off the bed and went to leave, but his hand clamped around her wrist.

His eyes sparked with devilment. "Did you just dare to threaten me?"

She should have stopped there, but her fiery temper got the better of her, and quickly raising her chin, she said mockingly, "Of course! Did you expect anything less?"

He drew her against his chest, and Bess had no choice but to look up at him. Lord, he was gorgeous. His eyes held hers, their intense hazel depths sending a jolt of desire racing straight through her. His sheer masculinity was almost overwhelming. She blinked quickly, trying to control her emotions, and attempted to break free, but she couldn't budge.

Annoyed, she furrowed her brows and spat, "Let me go this instant!"

"No, Bess. No one threatens me without consequences."

He moved so swiftly that Bess had no time to fathom what he was doing, and she soon found herself face down, over his lap, as he settled himself on the edge of the bed.

"What're you doing?" she shrieked.

"I'm going to give you a good spanking, sweet Bess. Something I think you need."

She struggled as he pulled her forward, but it made no difference. The man was enormous, and her strength was useless against his.

"You can't do this!" she protested.

"Oh, yes, I can. Bad girls get chastised, Bess, and your behaviour is most definitely bad."

"Bad? What did you expect? You captured me! I didn't even want to be here." She protested, trying to raise herself from his lap. He pushed her back down with one enormous hand, leaving it there for good measure so she couldn't move.

"I merely wanted to share a rum with you. You're the one who decided to throw a glass and have a tantrum."

Reaching beneath her, he expertly unlaced her breeches and pulled them down to her knees.

Bess opened her mouth to protest, but it turned to a gasp when his large hand landed firmly on her soft bottom.

"Ooooof!" Before she had time to recover, his hand came down again and again.

Before long, her bottom was on fire, each swat adding to the unbearable sting.

"Aow! Ouch! I hate you! Ooh! You're a beast! Ouch!"

He chuckled. "A beast, am I?"

He gave her two swats in quick succession, which made her yelp.

"You have a quick mouth on you, Bess."

Another two smacks left her squirming and biting her lip to contain her whimpers. She didn't want to give him the satisfaction of hearing her cries. Bastard. Big, sexy bastard. Good lord!

He stopped but left his hand on her sizzling bottom. The feeling was quite exquisite, and Bess could hardly think straight.

"So, if I pour you another glass of rum, do you agree to sit and talk rather than attack me?" He said.

She huffed and said indignantly, "I doubt I can sit now! Not comfortably, anyway."

She heard his deep laughter and looked over her shoulder at him. Her breath caught in her throat – Lord, he was such a handsome man. His dark hazel eyes looked down at her, and she could clearly see the laughter and strength within. It kindled a flame within her, and she found herself drawn to him like a moth to a flame.

"I think, my little firebrand," he grinned, "that you and I have the beginning of a wonderful relationship."

"Relationship?" She queried, frowning.

He moved swiftly. Turning her around and positioning her higher on the bed, he quickly joined her, his lips quickly claiming hers in a searing kiss.

Bess started to protest but found she couldn't. He was too exciting, too damn irresistible. His lips ground into hers, strong and demanding, yet coaxing at the same time.

A surge of excitement ripped through her, and when his hand moved downward to cup her bottom, she nearly swooned. She could feel the rigid, hard length of his manhood pressing into her belly, and of their own volition, her thighs widened, her breeches falling to her ankles. She kicked them off in a heartbeat.

When she felt his fingers slide over her slippery folds, it was exquisite. She had thought Julio was exciting, but Captain Bill was beyond compare. He pushed one finger into her, and she almost climaxed on the spot; it was so intense. His masterful lips moved lower, kissing her slender neck and then further down to her breasts. She arched her back, seeking a release from the heady excitement he was building inside, and when he moved her blouse aside and his mouth settled over one of her nipples, she gasped softly.

A part of her tried to resist, knowing that what she was doing was wrong on so many levels, but her desire for him was too strong. If she were to marry the boring Lord Fairchild, then she wanted to know what it was like to have a strong, virile man make love to her. Bedamned if anyone considered it unseemly or wrong! No one would ever know.

He left her for a moment to disrobe, his eyes never leaving hers. Their dark hazel depths claiming her for his own.

She felt the bed dip and the warmth of his strong body as he covered her once more. "You're beautiful, Bess. A treasure beyond compare."

She saw in his eyes an intensity that made her catch her breath, and when his lips claimed hers, she opened up to him like a flower in spring.

When she felt his manhood begin to penetrate her womanly core, she didn't stop him. She wanted him, and that was all that mattered.

Slowly, he pushed into her pliable body. She felt her sheath stretching to accommodate his girth, and then, with a firm thrust, he was fully in. She gasped a little and clung to his shoulders.

"You're a virgin?" He said, his tone a little shocked.

She whispered tightly. "Does it matter?"

"No, of course not. I'm just surprised, that's all."

He kissed her again and began to move his shaft steadily inside her. Bess began to feel her body respond to his. Tension began to build, and her small hands clung onto his shoulders until, with a cry of delight, she reached her pinnacle.

Bill continued thrusting his thick length into her lush body and then suddenly withdrew as he climaxed, ensuring there would be no unwanted consequences.

For a moment, they lay together without speaking, both coming down from the giddy heights of their love-making.

Raising himself up on one elbow, he looked down at her and said, "So Captain Bess, how is it that you were still a virgin, and more to the point, why didn't you tell me?"

Chapter Three

Captain Bill looked down into the sultry eyes of Captain Bess, watching the array of emotions wash over her face.

Had he known she was a virgin, he would have taken more care, but his desire for the beauty had driven him with a need far deeper than he had ever experienced. There was something about her. She was independent and fiery, and his need to tame her was overwhelming.

He trailed a finger down her chin, her neck, and further down to encircle one of her pert little pink nipples. It immediately hardened under his touch.

Drawing his eyes away from the tempting little morsel, he returned his gaze to hers. She was staring at him with a slightly guarded look.

"What secrets are you hiding, I wonder?" he asked her.

A becoming flush appeared on her cheeks, and her eyes flashed with a hint of anger. "The secrets I hold are mine. You have no need to know everything about me."

He smiled and reached for her hand, drawing it close to his mouth and kissing her knuckles. "Very well, sweet Bess. I won't pry. We all have our secrets."

Standing up and walking naked to the desk, he picked up the rum bottle and held it aloft. "Now, shall we have a drink before we part company?"

He noted she was quietly admiring his physique, and it heartened him. She was no shy, retiring wallflower. Bess was a feisty little firebrand that was a match for him in every way.

She smiled. "Yes, I'll take a rum with you, and I promise not to throw it at you this time."

"If you do, you know what happens."

He poured out two glasses and walked back to her, handing her one. She took a large mouthful and let the fiery liquid slip down her throat, closing her eyes. "Now that's a smooth one."

"Plundered from a merchant ship off France," he remarked.

He downed his in one go, and then, when she'd finished hers, he took the glass off her and put both on the floor before sweeping her into his arms.

Her eyes sparkled with devilment, and she said, "Why, Captain Bill, haven't you had enough?"

"No," he growled, "Not nearly enough!"

His lips claimed hers as he took her again to the giddy heights of satisfaction, her small cries music to his ears.

A while later, Bill swung Bess back onto *the Blue Belle,* where Cat and her crew were waiting anxiously for her to return.

Bess felt a little embarrassed that she had taken so long, but truly, she hadn't been able to help herself.

Cat went to step forward to drag her away from Bill's massive arms, but Bess raised a hand. "It's alright, Cat."

Gazing into her emerald eyes, Bill said softly, "Until next we meet, my sweet Bess. Then may the best captain prevail."

Before Bess could retort, his lips crushed down upon hers in a searing kiss that left her breathless. As quickly as he had come, Bill swung back across to *the Avalon* and began bellowing out orders to set sail.

Bess touched her fingers to her lips, still tingling from his kiss, and turned to find Cat gaping at her.

"What the hell, Bess?"

Bess blushed and smiled wryly at her friend. "Don't worry, Cat. Come into our cabin, and I'll explain everything." Turning to McGregor, who was staring at her as though she were mad, she told him, "Set a course for Jersey, McGregor."

"Will do." He walked off, mumbling, "Women!"

Bess laughed under her breath and suddenly felt a tug on her sleeve. Cat was looking at her with exasperation. "You have some explaining to do!"

When they were inside their shared cabin, Bess explained what had happened. When she finished, Cat was almost speechless.

"You gave yourself to him?"

"He gave himself to me as well. It works both ways. It was fun." She walked over to one of the lattice windows and stared out at the sea. "He's so handsome."

Cat gasped. "Oh, Lord. Have you lost your senses? What if you fall pregnant?"

Bess shook her head. "He was very careful not to let that happen." She looked embarrassed for a moment. "If you know what I mean?"

"I suppose we should at least be thankful for that!" Cat said, shaking her head. She glanced at Bess's dreamy expression and added, "You're not falling in love with the rogue, are you?"

"No, I don't think so. I just wanted to see what a real man felt like before getting married." She pulled a face. "Although maybe I have made things worse, what if Lord Fairchild is a terrible lover?"

"Well, I think Captain Bill has a bloody nerve! Taking your virginity like that was wrong."

"He didn't know."

Cat's eyes bulged. "You didn't tell him?"

"Well, I was lost in the moment. It didn't seem to matter. He didn't hurt me, if that's what you're worried about. Apart from the spanking, that is. That stung!"

Cat rolled her eyes to the heavens. "What am I going to do with you, Bess?"

Bess sniggered. "Nothing?"

Cat shook her head but smiled. "You're trouble; do you know that? But as long as you're unharmed, then I guess all is well."

"It is. So please don't worry about me."

"Do you think he'll come back into our territory again?"

Gazing out over the rolling seas, Bess replied softly, "Only time will tell. But one thing is certain: I'll meet him head-on if he does!"

And with that, she shot Cat a wicked look and laughed.

"You are a devil, Bess. Perhaps you and Captain Bill are a match that was meant to be!"

Two weeks later...

The Blue Belle dropped anchor in her secret cove along the south coast near Portsmouth, just as the sun dipped below the horizon. As the crew readied the tender, Bess paused on the deck, breathing the familiar scents of home. Dressed in her pale silken dress, she looked every bit like a refined lady.

"How long are you going back for?" Cat asked her.

"Two or three weeks, I suppose. How about you?"

"I'll do the same. We can meet up here around the end of July. Come and see me at the tavern when you get a free moment. Mr Clark would love to see you."

"I should love to."

Cat turned around and gave instructions to McGregor to return for them at the end of the month. McGregor would take *the Blue Belle* down to Cornwall, where a lot of the crew's family were located, so they could have a brief respite and spend their ill-gotten gains. There were many coves to hide in, and McGregor knew them all!

When Bess arrived at her home, Denby Manor, her father greeted her with a hug as she stepped out of the carriage.

"Elizabeth, my dear, so good to have you back! The country air has done you good, I see. You're looking quite radiant."

She flushed a little as her thoughts immediately went to Captain Bill. He had certainly made her feel radiant.

"Thank you, Papa."

"Lord Fairchild has been asking for you. I thought of giving him the address in Kent but then decided not to."

Bess's heart stopped for a moment. Good lord. She didn't want him to find out that she wasn't there. That could open up a whole can of worms.

"Thank you for not telling him, Papa. I would rather see him here. It's far more convenient, and it's also a long way for him to ride."

"Indeed, it is. You're very thoughtful, my dear."

She followed him up the grand steps and into the large hallway.

"Lovely to have you back with us, Miss Warren." Stiles, their butler, said, looking genuinely happy.

"Thank you, Stiles. Can you arrange for my luggage to be taken to my room?"

"Of course."

It always felt a little odd walking around on land. She got so used to her sea legs that coming home felt unusual.

"I'll order some tea. Do you want anything to eat?" her father asked as she followed him into the parlour.

"No, thank you; I'll wait until dinner tonight."

She sat down on one of the sumptuous sofas and leaned her head back against the plush fabric as she waited for her father to ring the bell for tea. When the maid had taken his order, her father said, "Your brother is coming to stay for a few days. He should arrive the day after tomorrow."

She sat forward and said, "Oh, it'll be lovely to see Adam."

Adam was older than her by five years and worked as a lawyer in London. They didn't get to see much of one another nowadays, but when they did, they always got along, for they had been close as children.

"I think I'll arrange for a little soireé, you know." Her father declared, "I'll invite Lord Fairchild to dinner as well. It'll be good for them to see each other again considering they will soon be brothers-in-law." He frowned. "Speaking of which, my dear, have you decided when you would like to get married? August is a delightful month, and one can normally guarantee good weather. What do you think?"

Bess swallowed hard. Good lord, this was all a bit sudden. She'd only been home a few minutes, and already he wanted to know her plans.

Smiling politely, she responded, "I'm not certain yet, Papa. Lord Fairchild and I will discuss it, and of course, you'll be the first to know."

"Of course, of course," he reasoned.

He chattered on about recent events in town, and Bess quietly listened, but her mind was elsewhere. Caught between two men, her mind was in turmoil.

The next day...

After a very comfortable sleep, Bess awoke to the sound of small pebbles hitting her bedroom window. Frowning, she threw the covers back, padded barefoot to the tall lattice windows, and looked down onto the drive.

"Adam!" she cried. She should have known. He used to do the same thing as a child to gain her attention.

She opened the window and called down to him. "Brother! I thought you weren't arriving until tomorrow."

He grinned. "You know me; I'm full of surprises!"

"I'll join you in the dining room. I won't be long."

Ringing the bell for her maid, she was soon washed and dressed in record time. Her hair was neatly pinned into a fashionable knot with side ringlets, and she rushed down the winding staircase, across the hallway, and into the dining room.

Adam stood up as she entered, and she walked over to kiss him on the cheek. Gazing at him warmly, she said, "It's so lovely to see you."

He was as handsome and dashing as ever, his dark hair swept back in a fashionable wave. He was over a head taller than her and had always teased her about her height. But mostly in good humour, unless they had one of their rare fights, which brothers and sisters are prone to.

"And you," he responded. "I can see the Kent air did you some good."

"Oh, yes. It was lovely. What brings you down to visit us? Business or purely pleasure?"

She reached for a piece of toast and slathered some butter on it while he spoke.

"Well, a bit of both, I suppose. I have an elderly client, Lord Fitzroy, who recently found out that he has a granddaughter. She was adopted at birth, and he wants me to find her."

"Oh, how exciting!" Bess said, "A real-life mystery." She bit into her toast whilst the maid poured a cup of coffee for her. "What happened to the girl's parents?"

"I don't know about the father but the girl's mother, Lord Fitzroy's daughter, died a few weeks ago. " He leaned forward in his seat. "Apparently she had the child out of wedlock and, fearing a scandal, gave the baby away. But, I guess, in a moment of remorse and knowing she was dying, she finally told her father about it."

"Oh, how sad. That little girl never got to see her mother. I wonder where she is now."

"Lord Fitzroy thinks she's somewhere in Portsmouth, hence the reason I've returned home for a while. It's a good way for me to see you and Father and do my work. So you see, this trip is both business and pleasure."

"And how lovely it is to see you. Maybe I can help you. I love a good mystery." Her eyes twinkled with excitement.

"You always had an inquisitive mind, so yes, any help would be most welcome." He leaned back in his chair and studied her. "It's been ages since I last saw you. I missed you."

She grinned. "And I you!"

"We'll have to make the most of this time together, that's for certain. Now, pass me a bit of that toast; I'm starving!"

Chapter Four

After a day spent relaxing with her brother and going through details about the missing child, the next day dawned with the rather daunting prospect of seeing her betrothed.

Bess pulled the coverlet up under her chin and almost had no desire to leave the comfort of the big bed.

Was she really going to go through with marrying Lord Fairchild?

Did she really want to spend her life with someone who didn't have any personality? A man who hadn't even tried to kiss her yet.

Her thoughts turned to Captain Bill, and she smiled wickedly. Oh, now there was a difference. She would never regret that night, ever. Her breath caught in her throat as she pictured his handsome face and solid, muscled body. Good Lord, what a man!

Her lip curled as a vision of Lord Fairchild came to mind. Oh, God!

Her father had arranged the marriage. He decided that she needed to marry into money, and that was something Lord Fairchild had plenty of. She had quite a bit saved up now, though, from her piracy pursuits, but it was all kept hidden. She did it more for the adventure, but the large stash she had accumulated was very satisfying.

Adam would inherit the family estate, and it would be his wife who benefited from it. So Bess needed a rich man with a big house to ensure her future comfort, or so her father kept insisting.

She stared at the ceiling, wondering if she was doing the right thing. If she married him, she wouldn't be able to keep her double life going without him knowing. And what if she had children?

Oh, dear me.

Ellen, her maid, arrived with some hot water for her morning ablutions, so reluctantly she slid from beneath the covers and began to get ready for the day. At least one thing was going to be interesting today, and that was accompanying her brother into Portsmouth to make enquiries for his client.

Portsmouth Harbour

The town was bustling with people when Bess and Adam alighted from their carriage.

"Good lord, it's almost as busy as London." Adam proclaimed, his lips curling in distaste.

Bess smiled and sucked in a lungful of the salty sea air. "Ah, it's so refreshing, though. Don't you just love the smell of the sea?"

Adam shrugged. "It's alright, I suppose." He said noncommittally, as was his way.

She shook her head at him and then asked, "Where shall we begin? Is there a shop or street that Lord Fitzroy mentioned?"

Adam reached inside his waistcoat and pulled out a piece of paper. He studied it for a moment and then said, "He mentions a place called Smedley's. It was an orphanage. But there's no mention of a street name. We'll have to ask around."

Bess sighed. "All these years, Lord Fitzroy's granddaughter has been out there unaware of her true heritage. Is he very rich?"

"Exceedingly!" Adam remarked. "And the thing is, he has no other heirs. I do hope the girl's still alive."

Just then, a weathered sailor hobbled by, humming an old sea shanty. Adam stopped him. "Excuse me, sir, but have you knowledge of an orphanage hereabouts called Smedley's?"

The man scratched his stubbled chin. "An orphanage, ye say? Well now, let me see." He looked down at the ground, thinking hard. "There was one by the old mill and another at the end of town. What was the name now? Might've been Smedley's, but I can't recall clearly."

"Which end of town would that have been?"

The sailor pointed up the road and said, "Not far up there. It was a big old house."

"You've been most helpful, Sir." Adam said. Reaching into his pocket, he handed the man a coin.

His eyes lit up, and his fingers quickly curled around the money before Adam could change his mind. "Thank 'ee, sir; most kind of ye."

When the man walked off, singing his shanty even louder than before, Adam turned to Bess. "At least we now know where to start. Come on."

Half an hour later, their hopes were dashed when they found out that Smedley's orphanage had changed ownership and was now called Thatcher's. There had been a fire ten years ago, and all records had been destroyed. Half the building had perished along with them. A rich benefactor had helped with the rebuild, but that didn't aid Adam in his quest.

He sighed heavily as they walked down the steps back onto the street. Bess linked her arm through his. "What should we do now?"

Adam shrugged. "Well, I think we should have lunch and then decide on our next move. Can you recommend a place to eat?"

"Indeed, I can, brother." Bess led him straight to Mr Clark's tavern. It would be lovely to see Cat and introduce her to her brother. In all the years they had known each other, there had never been an opportunity for them to meet. Either they were at sea or her brother was stuck in London, working.

To her delight, Cat was standing at the bar talking to Mr Clark. She beamed when she saw Bess. "Bess! How lovely to see you."

"Bess?" Adam said, puzzled.

"Oh, it's just a nick-name she uses for me." Bess quickly said, shooting Cat a warning glance. "Adam, let me introduce my friend Catherine Penley, or Cat for short."

"Cat, this is my brother, Adam."

Cat's eyes swept over her brother, and Bess saw an instant attraction. When she glanced at Adam, she could see it was mutual.

"Nice to meet you, Adam." Cat almost purred.

Adam bowed eloquently and said, "It is a pleasure to meet you."

His manners made Cat raise an eyebrow, and Bess stifled a giggle. "We've come to take lunch, Cat. Is there something nice on the menu today?"

"Roast beef and veg. Two plates?" She looked at them expectantly.

"That'll be lovely. Will you join us?" Bess asked her.

"Just try and stop me." She smiled and said, "I'll bring some wine as well."

She disappeared into a back room, leaving Bess and Adam to sit down at one of the free tables.

"She's very pretty." Adam said. "Why have I never met her before?"

"Because you're rarely at home. You spend far too much time up in London." She angled her head and asked, "Do you like her?"

"She's definitely caught my attention." He smiled wickedly.

It wasn't long before they were tucking into the meal, and with the wine flowing, the conversation was relaxed and amiable. Cat knew to certainly refrain from mentioning anything about *the Blue Belle* and their life as pirates. Adam was her brother, and even though they were close, she knew he would be horrified to know the truth about her clandestine activities.

Bess and Adam told Cat about their mission to find the orphan and shared their findings, or lack thereof, with her. As the story unfolded, Cat grew very quiet. When they finished, she looked pensively at Bess. "I know I'm most probably being a bit fanciful, but could I be the lost heiress you're looking for?"

Adam raised an eyebrow. "You were an orphan here in Portsmouth?"

She nodded. "I was adopted at a very young age by the Penleys, and I don't know my real surname. The orphanage told my adoptive parents that my mother had born me out of wedlock and, to avoid a scandal, had given me away. I've always wondered who she was." She shrugged. "But there are lots of babies given up for adoption every year." She sighed, smiling wistfully. "But to be an heiress, wouldn't that be something?"

Bess tapped her fingers on the table. "I had no idea you were adopted in Portsmouth. I thought your adoptive parents were from Devon?"

"They were, but they moved here, and that's when they adopted me."

"Well, I never. All these years, I never knew that! I just assumed you were from Devon too!" Her eyes lit up with excitement. "Maybe your idea is not so far-fetched, Cat. Someone has to be the heiress, and why not you?"

Adam rubbed his chin thoughtfully. "If birth documents were destroyed, we must find another way to prove lineage. Perhaps I could speak with your adoptive parents? They may remember something of import that was told to them at the time."

Cat shook her head. "Sadly, they both died when I was sixteen."

"Oh, I am sorry to hear that." Adam said, looking down at the table. 'This is all very frustrating. We have no leads at all."

"We need to find someone that worked at Smedley's before the fire." Bess suggested, "Maybe there's someone who would remember the Penleys adopting Cat and how she came to be there."

"Could I join you? With three of us on the case, we're bound to discover something – even if it means I find out I'm not going to be rich beyond my wildest dreams!" Cat said, rolling her eyes.

Adam raised his glass and said, "Very well. To us three, and hopefully, a wonderful outcome!"

That evening

Bess peered at herself in the mirror, hardly recognising the elegant woman in the reflection. Her hair was neatly swept up into a pretty knot, and elegant curls framed her face. Her dress was of the finest fabric in a shade of cream, and her necklace was a delicate line of pearls.

She looked every bit the perfect fiancée, or so she hoped to appear, to Lord Fairchild.

Ellen looked at her in the mirror. "You look stunning, Miss."

"Oh, thank you, Ellen." She picked up her fan from the dressing table and stood up. "Has Lord Fairchild arrived yet?"

"Yes, Miss. So have the other guests." She walked over to open the door for her. "Have a lovely evening, Miss."

Bess grinned and left the room, her skirts swishing elegantly as she descended the staircase.

When she stepped inside the drawing room, Lord Fairchild was the first to notice her. Smiling briefly, he walked over and, lifting her hand, kissed her knuckles. "My dear Elizabeth."

"My lord," she curtseyed politely. She hadn't seen him for a few months, but her heart didn't beat any faster or her pulse race from seeing him. No. He had no effect on her whatsoever.

"I would like to introduce you to a friend of mine." He said, drawing her over to the fireplace, where a tall, smartly dressed man was in conversation with her neighbours, Lord and Lady Hamble.

"Excuse me, William, but may I present my fiancée, Miss Elizabeth Warren?"

The man turned around, and Bess almost collapsed with shock. It was Captain Bill. But not as she had seen him on board *the Avalon*. No, this man was dressed in finely tailored clothes, his hair neat, and his boots highly polished. But those eyes! They looked at her keenly, the deep hazel depths sweeping over her intently, taking everything in.

Her heart stilled. Could it truly be him? Was she going mad? Imagining things? How could he be here?

But no, it was him—her rival, her captor, her secret passion. Captain Bill!

"My dear, you look a little startled." Lord Fairchild said, "I know William's size can seem intimidating, but I assure you, his bark is much worse than his bite."

"Indeed it is." Bill gave an eloquent bow and said, "Lord William Maidstone, at your service, ma'am."

Bess swallowed hard and croaked, "Pleased to meet you, my lord."

He smiled, and she detected a hint of humour in his tone when he said, "I had no idea your fiancée was so beautiful, Clarence."

He was keeping a veneer of civility, but in his eyes, she could see he had a thousand questions he needed answering. As did she!

"Yes, I am a lucky man." Lord Fairchild declared.

Her father joined them. "Dinner's about to be served, so if you follow me, we'll go to the dining room."

As the guests settled into their seats at the long, elegantly laid table, Bess found herself engaged in polite conversation with Lord Fairchild, her mind a whirlwind of conflicting thoughts.

It was so hard to remain focused when Captain Bill was sitting right opposite. Her eyes darted across the table, catching glimpses of him as he effortlessly charmed the other guests. His magnetic presence drew attention, and it was obvious he was equally at ease with society as he was with a pirate crew.

Bess couldn't help but steal glances, her heart torn between resentment and an undeniable attraction. Comparing him to Lord Fairchild was like chalk and cheese. They were totally different.

It didn't help that he was seated beside Lady Melissa Hamble, her neighbour's daughter, and he seemed to be paying her a lot of attention.

Melissa and Bess had been rivals for years, both as hot-headed as each other, which had led to many a confrontation.

Bess tried to convince herself that she wasn't jealous, but she was. She had no claims on Bill, and she knew she was being unreasonable, but her desire for him was so strong that when a ripple of jealousy surged through her slender body, she couldn't deny how she felt.

She caught Bill looking at her a couple of times, his eyes mocking hers when they met. Her eyes flashed angrily back at him, and his lips twitched in response, unperturbed.

As the evening progressed, Lord Fairchild, oblivious to the hidden turmoil, conversed with Bess, his voice tinged with excitement about their impending nuptials. Bess nodded and smiled, her thoughts elsewhere.

She couldn't shake the memory of the battle of wills, the stolen plunder, and the undeniable tension that simmered between her and Captain Bill. The man who had taken her virginity still had a claim on her heart.

As the evening drew to a close, Bess knew she had to speak with Bill before he left. She had too many questions, and she wanted them answered. But how could she get him alone without anyone knowing?

Chapter Five

The moon hung high in the night sky as the last of the guests departed. Bess had hoped to waylay Bill before he left, but Lord Fairchild had stuck to her like glue, and there had been no opportunity.

She stood outside in the silence, trying to control her emotions. Seeing Bill again and in such a fine setting had made her rethink her future.

Cursing under her breath, she leaned against a tree and rubbed her forehead. What was she going to do? Did she really intend to still go through with the marriage?

Too het up to go to bed, she walked through the moonlit garden. The scent of blooming flowers filled the air, mingling with the salty breeze from the nearby harbour. It was a beautiful evening, and after the stressful soirée, it was nice to just quietly reflect.

She was disappointed that she hadn't been able to speak with Bill, but she wasn't defeated, for their paths would surely cross again. Whether on land or at sea, she just knew they would meet.

Feeling resolute, she turned to make her way back towards the house. Just as she took her first step, a strong hand shot out from the shadows, snaking around her wrist. Startled, she gasped, but before she could react, she was pulled forcefully into the old stables nearby.

The dim light cast by a single lantern revealed Captain Bill's face, his eyes glinting with intent. Bess's heart raced, her breath catching in her throat as she found herself face-to-face with the man who had stirred within her a whirlwind of emotions.

"Bill," she breathed, her voice barely above a whisper. "I thought you'd left!"

He released her wrist, his hand lingering near her arm. "And yet, here we are," he replied, his voice low and filled with a hint of longing. "I couldn't leave without talking to you properly."

Bess's eyes searched his face, her heart aching with a myriad of unspoken desires. "What do you want to say?" she asked, her voice trembling with emotion.

He took a step closer, and the space between them filled with electric tension. "I want to know why you are engaged to a man you clearly do not love."

Her eyes widened. "What is it to you?"

He raised his hand and clasped her jaw, angling her face to his. "Because he will never satisfy you. You're far too willful to have a weak-minded man like him." His lips touched hers. "You need a firm hand, someone to satisfy your insatiable thirst, your hunger, and your need that lies within this beating heart." His hand moved down to her breast, cupping the sensitive mound. His other hand reached around and cupped her bottom, pulling her against his obvious arousal.

"I... you...!" Bess was finding it hard to speak, her heart pounding loudly in her chest.

Suddenly, his lips claimed hers. She surrendered to his expert touch, opening her mouth to accept his tongue as it fenced erotically with hers. Her whole body was on fire for him. He broke away, placing kiss after kiss on her slender neck and then turning her around in one lithe move; he moulded her body to his. She was so aroused that she could hardly concentrate. His breath moved her hair as he whispered in her ear. "You're mine, Bess."

She felt his hands on the hem of her dress, and she knew it was exactly what she wanted. And even if she had wanted to fight it, she couldn't. A draught of air hit her thighs as he threw her skirts over her back, and leaning her against some hay bales, he quickly drew her bloomers down to her ankles.

Her eyes shot open when she felt his hot breath on her womanhood. But when his tongue began an assault on her tender folds, she was lost. He pushed a finger inside her, and she climaxed almost instantly, her mind spiralling to the heavens.

Bill listened to her small cries of pleasure; it was music to his ears. Sitting across the table all night, he could think of nothing else.

Seeing her looking so resplendent in her finery and knowing her as the willful Captain Bess, his need to take her had almost overwhelmed him. How he endured dinner, he had no clue.

But now, the dark-haired beauty was in his arms, and she was his. He owned her, and he would make sure she knew it.

Quickly, he unbuttoned his breeches and released his pulsing manhood. He was so hard, it was almost painful. No woman had ever made him feel this way. His need for her was something far beyond the physical; it was mental as well. A need. A yearning.

He positioned himself at her entrance and, placing his hands on her hips, he guided himself slowly right up to the hilt. Her soft cries as he filled her almost made him climax, but he willed self-control.

Slowly and purposefully, he began to pump his hips against hers, drawing cries of delight from Bess, his feisty little pirate captain. She was perfection. His to have. His to hold.

Realising he was near completion, he reached around and played with her little nub until he felt her body tense and knew she had reached her pinnacle. He allowed himself a few more thrusts before withdrawing as he climaxed, his large body collapsing against her, replete and satisfied.

Bess leaned against the hay bale, fully satiated and hardly believing what had just happened. Bill turned her around and kissed her fully on the lips.

"God, I've been wanting to do that all evening." He growled, "I could hardly think of anything else."

Bess narrowed her eyes. "You didn't seem to have any problem concentrating when I saw you talking to Lady Melissa!"

He pulled back and looked into her eyes, then threw his head back, laughing. "Why, Captain Bess, I do believe you're jealous!"

"Shhhh! Someone will hear us," she warned him. "And no, I'm not jealous; I'm just pointing out how you lie so easily." In all truth, she was jealous, but she didn't want him to know that.

He nuzzled her neck. "I never lie, sweet Bess. In all truth, I could think of nothing else but your sweet body. Talking to others was the only way I could distract myself, but it wasn't easy."

Bess was having a hard time concentrating with his teeth grazing her delicate skin. She pushed him away a little and looked into his eyes.

"Why did you hide your true identity from me?" she asked.

Captain Bill's eyes glittered in the soft light. "For the same reason you did, I expect. I have my reasons, Bess."

"How do you know Lord Fairchild?"

"We knew each other as children, but when my father died, we lost contact, and as you know, I make my living in a rather unconventional way." He grinned, showing his even white teeth against his tanned skin. For a moment, Bess was mesmerised, but then she urged him to continue.

"I met up with him again in London about a year or so ago. He's become a rather serious man, but not unlikeable." His eyes grew dark. "But as for marrying him, my dear Bess, don't even think about it."

"It's not my wish, but my father's." She responded softly.

A bittersweet smile graced his lips as he gently cupped her face. "Would you marry me if I asked?"

She caught her breath. "Would you ask?"

His eyes were intense. "Yes, I think I would, but I cannot. Not at the moment. Things are too complicated."

"Does Lord Fairchild know you have a pirate ship?"

He shook his head. "And I trust you won't tell him?"

"No, I would never do that. We both have our secrets to maintain." She reached down to her ankles and went to pull her bloomers back up, but his hands covered hers.

"Not yet; I haven't finished with you yet, sweet Bess."

He drew her against his massive body and claimed her lips once again. Locked in his embrace, Bess knew that her life had taken an unexpected turn. Her path ahead was uncertain, but she knew that marrying Lord Fairchild was something she just couldn't go through with. Not now.

Captain Bill thrilled her to the very core and satisfied her desire for adventure. Anything less was unthinkable.

On the ride home, Bill couldn't help but think fate was on his side. His encounter with Bess had been quite a shock when she'd been introduced to him as Miss Elizabeth Warren. For one moment, he thought he was imagining things, but then he saw that flash of fire in her eyes, and he knew immediately that she was most definitely his defiant little Bess.

How they had both kept cool heads, he had no idea. Dinner had been arduous when all he wanted to do was plough his length into her sensual body. He grew hard at the thought and shifted uncomfortably in the saddle.

He had told her he would come again tomorrow night, after midnight, when the household would be asleep. He wanted to tell her the circumstances of his life and why he had become Pirate Bill, and he wanted to hear her story as well, but only if she wanted to reveal it. He wouldn't push her.

His own path to piracy had almost been forced upon him. His father was addicted to gambling, and after losing his wealth, he was unable to pay his taxes. The government had taken everything—his land, his house—and in so doing, Bill had lost his inheritance. He still had his title, for what it was worth.

His face darkened as he remembered those dark days. His father had disappeared up north to stay with his aunt. They had never been close. He always felt his father blamed him for the death of his mother when she had given birth to him.

His father hadn't lasted long after that. He drank himself into oblivion and died the following year.

That was seven years ago. He was only twenty-seven at the time and had no real trade or profession to speak of, thus forcing him to sell most of his possessions before the bailiffs could seize them. This enabled him to fund the purchase of *the Avalon,* a sixth-rate frigate complete with guns and crew.

He had taken to his newfound vocation like the proverbial duck to water, with very few regrets. Granted, there were a number of occasions where he'd wondered what the hell he'd got himself into, but the excitement and adventure, not to mention the booty, made everything all worthwhile.

He'd spent much of the last seven years along the east and Gulf coasts of North America and much of the Caribbean, hunting ships and dodging privateers, as well as that constant thorn in his side, the US and Royal Navy.

Recently, though, his thoughts had been turning to hearth and home, yearning for longer than he'd care to admit to himself for sentiments of a more refined way of life. Perhaps settle down a little and purchase an estate? He certainly could afford one. Who knows? Maybe even get married and raise a family; he was the right age to do so.

So he had begun to plunder ships along the Bay of Biscay and up to the English Channel, which allowed him time to spend ashore and ingratiate himself into society once again as Lord Maidstone.

Time away had lessened the scandal surrounding his family name, and his commanding presence alone seemed to quell any gossip. In that, he had been most fortunate.

Thinking about his double life made him wonder why Bess did the same. What had made Miss Elizabeth Warren become a pirate? He thought about her fiery nature.

What a perfect wife the ravishing little beauty would make! The thought made him smile.

But how would he explain his past? It would be bound to come out sooner or later, so he couldn't keep it hidden. His family name had been dragged through the gutter; what parent would consent to his daughter marrying into that?

So that's why he had agreed to meet with Bess the next night, eager to unburden himself and reveal the circumstances that had led him down this path.

However, as fate often does, it intervened with a cruel twist. Upon arriving home at his small, rented house by the port, Bill found his quartermaster waiting for him, a grave expression etched on his face.

"Captain," he began, his voice laced with urgency, "we have a problem. Customs officials have been spotted along the coast."

Bill's heart sank, realising the implications of their unwelcome presence. "Bastards!" He spat. "How far away are they?"

"Not far at all. But we have enough time to sail out. The tide's on our side, and there's a stiff westerly. That's why I came. I think we must leave straight away."

The consequences of discovery would be dire for both him and his crew. *The Avalon* was no longer safe.

"We have no choice," Bill stated, his voice firm. "We'll set sail immediately."

Within half an hour, he was on deck. His crew had already begun the preparations to set sail, and it wasn't long before *the Avalon* was leaving her mooring and setting off out toward the channel.

Bill stood at the helm, his face grim and his thoughts consumed by the promise he had made to Bess. The disappointment and heartache he would cause by not showing up for their meeting weighed heavily on him. He had hoped for an opportunity to explain and perhaps build a future together. But fate seemed determined to keep them apart.

The Avalon, with the weight of the wind behind the sails, glided silently through the softly rolling waves into the inky darkness of nightfall.

Chapter Six

The next day

The sun rose over the horizon, casting its warm glow upon Bess's bedroom. She awoke with a smile on her face, blinking sleepily as she faced the bright light. Good lord, what dreams she had! They'd been full of Captain Bill and his roving hands. She blushed at the memory.

She sat up in bed, her eyes sparkling with excitement. Her heart was still fluttering with the memory of her encounter with him last night. She still found it hard to believe that he had a title.

She couldn't wait to tell Cat all about it. They had planned to meet up at the tavern again today, along with Adam, so they could further research the case for the lost heiress.

She just hoped she could concentrate properly because the anticipation of seeing Bill again after midnight was overwhelming.

Ellen arrived to help her dress and couldn't help but notice how happy she looked. Bess quickly explained that it was because she was going to spend the day with her brother.

"Oh, how lovely, Miss," she said whilst folding Bess's nightgown. "He's grown very handsome. I think he won't have any problems finding a wife."

"Indeed not", and if Bess had her way, it would be to her best friend, Cat. She had already witnessed the attraction between them, so it would be lovely if they could actually become attached.

As the day unfolded, Bess found herself more engrossed in her brother's case than she had thought, and she was quite thankful for the distraction. Adam had discovered the addresses of two elderly women who had worked at Smedley's during the time that Cat had been there.

So, together, the three of them took a carriage to the first address. After speaking with the woman, they came away none the wiser.

"She seemed a little addle-brained, or was it just me?" Cat said, pulling a face.

"I think that's putting it politely," Adam said. "She was clearly drunk. Did you see the bottles of ale on the kitchen table?"

"She wasn't much use, was she?" Bess remarked. "Maybe the next woman will be able to help."

"I hope so." Adam said as they reached the carriage. The driver opened the door for them, and Bess couldn't help but notice the way her brother gallantly helped Cat up the step.

Oh, yes, there was something developing there; she was certain of it.

The next address seemed abandoned when they walked up. The door was off its hinges, and there was a hole in the downstairs window. Cat grimaced. "Surely no one lives here, do they?"

"There is only one way to find out," Adam said, stepping forward. He tapped his cane on the half-open door.

"Hello? Anyone there? Mrs Thorpe?"

They looked at each other and went quiet, listening intently. A few minutes later, to their surprise, a woman hobbled up to the entrance.

"Yes?" she snapped, her eyes beady and wary.

"Good day, are you Mrs Thorpe?" Adam asked.

"Yes, what of it?"

Bess hid a smile. The woman was brusque and to the point. It looked like she wasn't about to take any nonsense.

Adam used his best charm. "My name is Adam Warren, and I'm a lawyer from London. I have been told that you used to work for an orphanage in town called Smedley's."

"Yes, what of it?" She snapped, drawing her shawl tighter around her shoulders, and her eyes regarding him with suspicion.

"I wondered if you were witness to a baby girl being left there by her mother."

She stepped back and shot him a look of annoyance. "Well, of course I was. Several of the poor little blighters! It's an orphanage; that's what 'appens!"

"Oh," Adam said, looking a bit defeated.

Cat stepped forward and said, "Pardon me, but do you remember any of the women that dropped these babies off? I mean, would you remember any names or their appearance?"

Mrs Thorpe's eyes softened as she looked at Cat, immediately warming to her. "Well, now. Would ye like to come in, and I'll see what I can recall."

"As long as it's not too much trouble." Cat said, smiling.

"Of course not, dearie. Come in."

When they turned their backs, Adam looked at Bess and whispered, "We won't catch anything in there, will we?"

Bess nudged him in the side. "Who cares! If we want to find out what she knows, we don't have a choice. Now, move, brother!"

Once inside, Mrs Thorpe walked over to a cabinet and opened a drawer. "I know it's in 'ere somewhere. Let me see." She rummaged around, tutting and grumbling to herself, before pulling out a small tin. "Ah, I knew I still 'ad it."

She walked over towards a small table, and placing the tin on the surface, she prised the lid off. It took a bit of effort, as the tin appeared to be quite rusty. "I kept a few trinkets from the babes when they were 'anded over to the orphanage. Old Samuel, the caretaker, would steal anything and everything, so I kept these little bits to one side so 'e couldn't get 'is thieving 'ands on 'em."

"What were you going to do with them?" Adam asked.

Bess was thinking the same thing. Wasn't she just as much a thief as 'Old Samuel'?

"I 'adn't intended to keep them, like. But when Smedley's caught fire, I grabbed everything I could. And then the place closed down. So I just kept it safe. It's been 'ere ever since."

She sat down and put the tin on her lap. "Now let me see what's in 'ere. Ah yes." She held up a little lock of hair, tied together with a cream ribbon. "She was a pretty little thing. She was adopted within a week of arriving." Then she held up a little silver rattle. "This belonged to a boy. A man dropped 'im off, saying 'e couldn't afford to keep 'im. Poor little sod."

Then she held up a small locket on a chain. "This was from a baby girl. I think it 'as a little cameo inside." She handed it to Cat. "See if ye can open it; my old 'ands are too gnarled for something so delicate."

Cat ran her fingers over the fine filigree chain and the delicate oval locket. "It looks very well made."

She opened it, and when she saw the painting inside, her eyes widened. Bess, looking over her shoulder, exclaimed, "Why, Cat – she looks like you!"

Adam took it from her hand and peered at it more closely. "The resemblance is uncanny." He looked back at Mrs Thorpe. "I presume this was the mother?"

"Let me 'ave a look."

He handed the locket back to her, and, squinting her eyes, she studied the cameo. "Oh, yes. That's 'er. A beautiful woman. She was most upset to leave the babe but said she 'ad no other choice." She sat back in her seat. "She was crying. Some of them don't cry. With some, ye can see the relief on their faces when they realise they 'ave one less mouth to feed. But this one was different. She came from money; ye could see it in her fine clothes and the way she 'eld herself."

Cat wiped away a tear. "I hate this damned society. What does it matter if a child is born out of wedlock? It's not fair!"

Bess placed her hand on her sleeve. "Perhaps we can make things right now, all these years later."

Adam nodded. "Oh, indeed, we can." He looked at Mrs Thorpe. "May we keep this locket?"

"Yes, I 'ave no use for it. It's been 'ere for all this time, just sitting in the tin. If it brings someone 'appiness, then I will be 'appy for it."

As the three of them returned to town in the carriage, Adam said, "I'll go to London and speak with Lord Fitzroy. He has portraits on his wall of his daughter, and I need to see if this cameo is the same. If it is, then I will arrange for you to meet with him, Cat. After that, it's up to you."

"Thank you. I think I need a drink after all that. My head is spinning."

"Shall we go to the tavern?" Bess asked.

"I don't need asking twice," Adam said, grinning.

What a revelation today had been! Smiling happily, Bess wondered if tonight would be just as revealing when Captain Bill would explain his double identity. The thought of meeting him again gave her cheeks a rosy hue, and she did her utmost to quell the surge of desire that shot through her. But it was hard!

When they had finished dinner and Adam had excused himself for a moment, Bess leaned forward and told Cat what had happened the previous night.

She clapped a hand over her mouth, her eyes wide. "You had Captain Bill at your dining table?"

"I know! I couldn't believe it either, and then when I found out he was Lord William Maidstone, I was astonished! I mean, Cat, he has a title; who would have believed it?"

"This is news indeed. I don't quite know what to say." She looked over her shoulder to make sure Adam wasn't in the vicinity and said, "Weren't you worried he would reveal who you were?"

"At first, but then I realised that we were both in disguise. If he said anything, then so would I!" She smiled wickedly. "Besides, who would believe that sweet Elizabeth Warren would do such a thing?"

Cat tilted her head and studied her. "Did you get to talk with him in private?"

"I might have!" Bess grinned.

Cat gasped. "You did it again, didn't you?"

"Yes. I can't deny it. Am I very bad, Cat?" She chewed her lip. "I just can't resist him."

"Who would have thought the fiery Captain Bess would give in so easily to such a man as Pirate Bill?"

"I didn't give in that easily!" She defended herself.

"You did!" Cat laughed. "But in all honesty, he is a very handsome man who could charm the birds off the trees. So I don't blame you, but I would advise caution." She frowned. "Are you still going to marry Lord Fairchild?"

"I don't think I can, you know, Cat. Comparing the two of them together last night was quite eye-opening." She looked despondently down at the table. "I will have to tell my father that I don't want to go ahead with the marriage. He's not going to like it, but it is my life, isn't it? And I think I'd rather just live life out at sea, to be honest, and remain single."

"Me too. The thought of marrying someone just for society's sake is quite alarming. The more time I spend at sea, the more appealing it becomes. At least, out there, we control our own destiny."

Bess raised her glass. "To us, my dear friend, and perhaps a life as spinsters!"

"You two are still in high spirits, I see." Adam said, returning to the table. "As well you should be. We have all worked jolly hard today." He raised his glass and said, "Chin chin!"

Bess caught Cat's eye across the table as they all chinked their glasses together. It was lovely having a friend and confidante like Cat. They were so in tune with each other, and she knew they would always look out for one another, no matter what life threw at them.

That evening...

As the hours passed, Bess's excitement for her upcoming meeting with Bill grew. She had sat through dinner with her father and Adam, doing her best to join in the conversation, but it was hard to concentrate.

Luckily, neither seemed to notice, for they were too preoccupied with Lord Fitzroy's quest and what it could mean for Cat. Her father was fond of Cat, but who wouldn't be? She had a lovely disposition.

The time was now fast approaching midnight, and dressed in one of her best gowns, Bess silently made her way down the stairs and into the gardens, being careful not to awaken her sleeping family. Taking a lantern, she trod the path towards the old stables and quickly snuck inside to wait for Bill.

An hour later, he still hadn't turned up. She yawned and walked to the entrance for the hundredth time, peering out to see if she could see any shadows or movement. But there was nothing.

Where was he?

Surely he wouldn't have stood her up deliberately? Would he? Her bottom lip began to tremble, and she blinked furiously to stop the tears from falling. No, he had seemed so sincere last night. Their connection to one another was true, surely?

She waited another hour, and still nothing. An owl hooted loudly, making her jump, but other than that, the night air was still.

Slowly, she felt anger begin to build in the pit of her stomach and rise up until, curling her hands into fists by her side, she admitted to herself that he wasn't coming.

He had got what he wanted last night and moved on. What had she expected from a man such as Bill? His reputation should have told her. He plundered other ships just as he had plundered her body. She could kick herself for being so gullible.

"I hate you, Bill!" She said in a low voice, "If I see you again, you will rue the day! I'll blow your ship out of the water! I'll... oh, I don't know what I'll do, but one thing's for certain... you won't do this to me again."

Picking up the lantern, she returned to the house, feeling as miserable as she could possibly be.

Chapter Seven

Captain Bill had managed to give the customs men the slip. It had been a close call, but nothing they weren't used to. With the wind in their favour, they swiftly fled the cove before they were even spotted. His crew was always on alert, and it usually paid off.

They had been at sea for a few days now, and the men were getting restless for a skirmish. Bill likened it to a lack of action, and the signs were obvious—less banter among the crew and the odd skirmish below deck.

The holds were empty and in dire need of another ship's bounty. Bill rubbed his hands together and gave a wicked smile as he contemplated the prospect of taking another prize. Oh yes, he could already feel the adrenaline pumping through his veins at the very thought. Easing himself up from his chair, he lifted his jacket from the hook and shrugged it on before striding from his cabin and stepping onto the deck.

Alec was already there, looking a little worse for wear, and Bill slapped him on the shoulder. "Had a bit too much of the old grog last night, did you?"

Alec winced and replied, "Aye, you could say that!"

Bill laughed, showing no sympathy. Alec was well known for being a hard drinker, so as it was all self-inflicted, he only had himself to blame. Besides, he was old enough and ugly enough to handle it!

It was a clear dawn on the open ocean, and striding over to the helm, Bill took out his spyglass and raised it to the horizon, looking for prey.

Soon, a merchant vessel hove into view. He studied it for a while, calculating its speed and size. Nodding with satisfaction, he decided it could be laden with rich cargo.

"Got us a live one, Alec. Hoist the colours; let's at 'em!" Bill cried. At his command, Alec bellowed to the crew, and within seconds, the ship was a hive of activity, the sails billowing as *the Avalon* bore down on the merchant ship.

Even from that distance, Bill could see they had noted the dreaded pirate flag and were now scrambling around in a panic. His eyes narrowed wickedly as he lowered the spyglass. He could feel the adrenaline flow through him and revelled in it.

As their prize drew closer, Bill gave the order to fire shots across her bow.

He was never quite sure what gave him the most pleasure—the sound of the cannon, the harsh smell of gunpowder, or the raucous approval of his crew.

Grappling hooks were quickly deployed, drawing the vessels together in a fusion of wood and iron. Bill and his cohorts entered the fray. The merchant crew fought as well as they could but were no match for *the Avalon* and her company as they stormed the deck.

A fierce scrum ensued, blades flashing in the sun. Bill fought like a man possessed, felling foe after foe with uncanny skill. But he enjoyed every minute.

Suddenly, out of the corner of his eye, he spied a merchant sailor aiming a pistol at one of his men, who was completely unaware.

With a roar, Bill threw himself at the man, hoping to push the pistol from his hands, but the man turned at the last minute and fired, more out of terror than anything. The shot hit a wooden mast right next to Bill, and the impact shattered the wood.

Bill winced and turned at the last minute, but even so, he suddenly felt a searing pain in his leg. Looking down, he saw blood on his thigh, but he had no time to dwell on his wound. The sailor was reaching for his sword, his face triumphant that he had managed to wound the pirate captain.

Bill, incensed, lunged again for him, only this time he had the upper hand, and lifting the man up as though he weighed nothing, he threw him overboard, watching with immense satisfaction as his arms flailed wildly around during his descent to the frothing sea below.

A few moments later, he heard the triumphant shouts of his crew—the battle was won and the ship captured.

Three days later

Bill, wounded and bedridden, lay in his cabin aboard *the Avalon*, becoming more and more frustrated as each day passed.

The battle with the merchant ship had taken its toll, and during the skirmish with the merchant sailor, a shard of wood had become lodged in his thigh, causing him great discomfort. The ship's surgeon, Patterson, had declared him out of action, insisting that he remain abed until he had fully healed.

Bill threw the covers back and looked at his thigh. He was lucky to have such a great surgeon like Patterson on board. His experience was exactly why he had hired him in the first place, and it had proved invaluable on many occasions.

He lifted the gauze dressing and winced as he looked at the bloodied, three-inch-long wound. Patterson had sewn the flesh together after delicately retrieving the wooden shard, and Bill had only managed to bear the pain due to several large mouthfuls of rum. But he could see Patterson had done a fine job. It just hurt like hell, and Patterson had demanded that he remain in bed until it was healed. The less movement, the better, apparently.

He scowled, and his jaw tightened with frustration. He had hoped to sail back to England and fulfil his promise to Bess—to explain why he led his double life. He knew without a doubt that she would already be angry with him for failing to turn up that night, but he had hoped to see her sooner rather than later to explain. The longer he left it, the more hostile she would be—he knew that with certainty.

Thinking about his sweet Bess made him even more frustrated. He longed to be by her side, to kiss her soft, pliable lips, and to plunge himself into her soft, willing body. His cock stiffened at the thought, and he shifted uncomfortably. There was nothing wrong with that part of his body; he chuckled to himself. That was clearly evident.

Leaning his head back against the pillows, he sighed heavily. Well, one consolation was that the merchant ship had been loaded with a full cargo. All manner of spices, fabrics, and, best of all, rum and wine were now safely in Bill's hold. So his crew was happy. They were, even now, en route to France to sell their bounty.

So as much as Bill was happy with the outcome, the pain in his leg served as a constant reminder of the distance that now separated him from his sweet, fiery Bess.

Woodleigh Manor

Adam sat opposite Lord Fitzroy in his luxurious wood-panelled study and watched him carefully as he studied the locket Mrs Thorpe had given them.

"It is a delicate piece of jewellery, but I don't recognise it." Lord Fitzroy said, turning it over in his hands.

"Perhaps you'll recognise the cameo inside?" Adam suggested. He was hopeful that it would unlock the truth of Cat's lineage.

Lord Fitzroy, his eyes filled with curiosity and a hint of scepticism, opened the locket and peered at the tiny picture. "Hmmn, the blasted thing's far too small to see properly."

He pulled open a drawer and drew out a large spyglass. Raising it to his right eye, he peered again at the cameo.

Adam held his breath and waited. Would it be the response he was waiting for? Or just another dead end?

Lord Fitzroy nodded slowly and then looked at Adam sharply. "This is my daughter. There is no doubt."

Adam slowly began to breathe again. "Then it looks as though we have found your granddaughter."

"It would seem that way. Come, I'll show you my daughter's portrait again, and you can see for yourself."

He led the way out of the study, walked across the large entrance hall, and then up the wide staircase. He stopped at a picture and pointed at it.

"There, you see."

Adam gasped. He had seen the portrait before, but seeing it again, he realised that she was the spitting image of Cat. He looked at Lord Fitzroy and said, "Her daughter looks just like her."

A mixture of emotions crossed the nobleman's face. "This has given me hope, my boy. When I first gave you the task, I thought it would be like searching for a needle in a haystack, but you have proved otherwise."

"I can hardly believe it myself."

"Bring her to me," he said, his voice filled with a hint of caution. "I will meet this young woman and ascertain for myself if she is who we think she is."

Adam, buoyed by Lord Fitzroy's response, nodded eagerly. The prospect of reuniting Cat with her rightful family filled him with a sense of purpose and excitement.

"I will arrange a meeting for this afternoon, if that would suit you, my lord."

"Indeed. The sooner, the better."

Adam left Lord Fitzroy's vast mansion with a spring in his step. What a revelation that meeting had been, and he couldn't wait to tell Cat and his sister.

Denby Manor

Bess sat opposite her father in the parlour and winced as she watched him pace the room.

"It's not so bad, Papa."

"Not so bad!" He said, rounding on her. He lifted his finger and pointed it at her angrily. "You have just told me that you have no wish to marry Lord Fairchild, an esteemed member of society, a man of social standing! Not so bad, you say?!"

"But Papa...!"

"Don't try and wheedle your way out of this. I cannot believe you would declare such a thing. Have you any idea the shame you will bring upon the family by annulling the engagement? Have you?"

Bess winced and hunched her shoulders. "Well, of course I do, but surely you would rather I was happy?"

"Penniless and happy? I don't think so. Lord, what on earth are you thinking?" He glared at her.

"But I don't love him."

"So? Love won't keep you warm when the weather's cold outside! Love won't pay the bills or keep food on the table!"

"But...!"

He interrupted her. "Get out of my sight. I need time to think about this."

Bess's eyes widened. He had never spoken to her in such a tone before, and tears welling up in her eyes, she quickly did as he bid, not wishing to anger him any further. Good lord. What a mess!

She rushed up the stairs and headed into her bedroom, slamming the door behind her. Leaning her back against the wood, she let the tears slip down her cheeks. She hated seeing her father so upset, but she would stand firm. She couldn't marry Lord Fairchild.

The assignation she had shared with Captain Bill had shown her how exciting life could be, and a life stuck with Lord Fairchild would end up killing her one way or another.

Even knowing that Captain Bill had forsaken her wouldn't change her mind. She realised that she wanted to marry for love, not for wealth or a place in a higher society. She had her own wealth stashed away, and if need be, she would remain single for the rest of her life.

One thing was certain, though. The next time she ever saw Captain Bill, she was going to make sure to make his life a misery.

Woodleigh Manor stood tall and imposing as Cat stepped out of the carriage onto the gravel drive. She looked up at it in awe, turning wide eyes to Adam. "I had no idea the estate was so big!"

Adam smiled at her. "I did try and tell you." He held his arm out, and she slipped her hand through. "Don't be alarmed," he added. "He is a serious man but kind."

He led her up the steps and was about to knock when the doors swung open. Lord Fitzroy himself stood there, ready to greet them.

Cat stared at him, feeling just a tad intimidated but keeping her gaze on him. He was a distinguished-looking man with silver hair and piercing blue eyes that held a glimmer of familiarity. He studied her back just as intently.

Adam looked from one to the other and broke the silence. "Lord Fitzroy, may I introduce Miss Catherine Penley?"

Cat curtseyed gracefully.

Lord Fitzroy gave an imperceptible nod. "Welcome, my dear. Come inside. I think we have rather a lot to discuss."

Cat's voice trembled slightly as she replied, "Thank you, Lord Fitzroy. It's an honour to be here." This was all a little overwhelming, but she knew she had to find out if she was truly related to him.

"Would you rather I stay in the carriage whilst you two discuss everything? I don't wish to intrude." Adam said, hesitating to step inside.

Cat immediately reached out and clutched his hand. "No, please, I would rather you stay."

He looked at her, and between them there was an understanding. "As you wish."

The meeting that followed was filled with questions, stories, and a shared exchange of memories. Lord Fitzroy recounted tales of her mother's past and what sort of woman she was.

Cat listened intently, realising her mother had the same wayward spirit as her own. Her heart yearned to have met her, but life wasn't always how one wanted it to be.

As the hours melted away, Cat and Lord Fitzroy discovered unexpected similarities in their personalities, and when he showed her the portrait of her mother, they both understood with certainty that Cat was indeed his long-lost granddaughter.

"She is so like you, Ca—" Adam went to use her familiar name but then changed his mind. "Miss Penley."

Cat eyed him with a twinkle in her eye that Lord Fitzroy never noticed. "There is such a resemblance that our connection cannot be doubted." She turned to Lord Fitzroy. "Do you know who my father was?"

"No, my dear. I did ask your mother, but she never revealed his name to me. But it matters not. You are my granddaughter; that's all we need to know."

As they parted ways, both Cat and Lord Fitzroy carried a newfound sense of purpose. Cat, filled with amazement that she had found her family roots, and Lord Fitzroy, driven by the desire to reclaim what he had lost.

Cat sat opposite Adam as their carriage began the journey home. She was so glad he had been with her today. He had an inner strength that she had come to admire. Perhaps more than she cared to admit. She had always vowed never to become attached. She had seen too many hearts broken over the years, yet this man was already getting under her skin.

She stared out of the window and watched the countryside pass by, quite in awe of how her life could change in so little time.

Chapter Eight

Bess had kept to her room for the rest of the afternoon, not wishing to rile her father even more. Keeping out of his way was the best plan, as far as she could tell. If he insisted she marry Lord Fairchild, then she would just have to sail away on *the Blue Belle* and never return.

But she truly didn't want to do that. She would miss everyone too much.

Dinner time arrived, and her maid, Ellen, came to see her. "Your father asks if you're joining him for dinner, Miss."

"Yes, I better had. He's riled up enough as it is, and if I don't appear, he'll accuse me of sulking!" She stood up and walked over to the dressing table. "Has my brother returned yet?"

"Yes, his carriage arrived a little while ago."

"Oh, marvellous. Help me change, Ellen, and do something with my hair, please!"

She was soon looking respectable, and taking a deep breath, she headed downstairs to the dining hall.

Her father gave her a cursory glance when she entered, and she realised he was still mad at her. Adam, however, greeted her warmly. "I got on favourably well with Lord Fitzroy today," he declared. "In fact, so much so that I took Cat to meet him this very afternoon!" He grinned, knowing his words would astound her.

"You did?" Bess exclaimed happily. "Good lord, that progressed quickly. So, what happened? Is she definitely related to him?"

Adam nodded. "Yes. One look at that portrait was enough to know. As we surmised in that small cameo, she is the spitting image of her mother."

"Oh, I am so pleased for her."

"At least someone's happy." Her father remarked.

Adam looked at him and then back to Bess, noticing the way her expression had quickly become veiled. "Has something happened that I should know about?"

"Ask your sister." Her father said, shooting her a look of disapproval.

Bess scowled. "If you must know, I have decided that I no longer wish to marry Lord Fairchild."

Adam looked at her askance. "But I thought it was all planned?"

"As did we all," their father said pointedly.

"Have you told him?" Adam asked her.

"Not yet. But I will."

Stiles, the butler, entered the room. "Are you ready for service, sir?"

Her father nodded, and they all took a seat at the dining table. Adam looked a little uncomfortable but did his best to make conversation as each course arrived.

On the dessert course, their father made his excuses and left the room. Adam immediately rounded on Bess. 'Whatever were you thinking? Why don't you want to marry Lord Fairchild?"

"I don't love him; that's why, and I don't wish to spend the rest of my life with someone who doesn't make me happy."

Adam rubbed a hand over his chin. "As much as I commiserate, why did you ever agree to marry him in the first place?"

She didn't want to tell him about Captain Bill. Good lord, he'd have a fit! So she just said, "Well, I've just come to realise that there's more to life than money or status."

Adam stared at her silently, taking in what she'd just said. "Well, while I do admire your honesty, Elizabeth, I wouldn't be at all surprised if you get shunned by society when you tell the poor man your decision."

He held his hand out to her across the table. "But I'm here for you if you need a shoulder to cry on, and also, know that you will always have a home here."

Bess smiled warmly and said, "You are such a dear brother. But what if your future wife wants me to leave?"

"That will never happen."

She looked at him and knew it to be the truth. He was strong in so many ways, and she was relieved to have him for a brother. Feeling somewhat content, she wondered how she was going to break the news to Lord Fairchild.

A week or so later, the day Bess had been dreading arrived, and Lord Fairchild came to visit.

Taking him into the parlour, she waited for him to sit down and then broke the news to him as gently as she could.

For a moment, his face went white, and then a deep red suffused his cheeks. He stood up and stared at her, his lips tight with anger. "May I ask why?"

Bess took a deep breath. "I find that I don't love you anymore. I am sorry for it, but I would rather be truthful with you." She held her hand out. "And I assure you, it is through no fault of your own."

"Oh, I don't doubt that for a moment." He sneered.

She allowed him that, for she could see her words had truly hurt him, but his next comment riled her.

"I gather you have taken a lover."

"Pardon?"

"Oh yes, don't think I didn't know. I was willing to forgive you, but now I won't."

Bess's heart dropped. "What do you mean?"

"Do you think I don't have my spies, my dear?" He tapped his fingers on the table. "Lord Maidstone was seen going into the stables with you. Do you deny it?"

Bess gulped. Of course, she was going to deny it! And strongly as well! "I have no idea what you're talking about!"

"Of course, you don't." He looked at her with eyes of steel. "You will regret this. I will make sure of it."

"There's no need to be like this."

He turned on her. "Oh, yes, there is. I was willing to forgive you for that indiscretion. Your beauty was worth it. But not now. I will make sure to let everyone know what a slattern you truly are."

"But it's not true!"

"Too late, my dear."

Bess watched him go and stood silently in shock. Oh, good lord! What had just happened?

Bess immediately had her horse saddled and rode to town to see Cat at the tavern. Her mind was in turmoil. She had never thought Lord Fairchild would show such a nasty side to his character. As much as she was dismayed at his threats, she was just as relieved to know that she had made the right decision.

The thought of having him as a husband made her shudder.

Cat greeted her with a big smile, which quickly faltered when she saw Bess's grim expression.

She quickly drew her to one side, away from the throng of customers. "What is it, Bess? What's happened?"

Bess explained her conversation with Lord Fairchild, and Cat's jaw dropped. "Oh my! What an absolute blaggard!"

"I don't know what to do." Bess confessed. "I don't want to stay home and find out everyone knows about Bill and me! I can deny it as much as I like, but people being people, they will just believe anything they're told!"

Cat grimaced. "You speak the truth. Lord Fairchild is so influential." She paced the room, and then suddenly, she placed her hands on her hips and declared, "Then let's not stay here! Let's sail away on *the Blue Belle* before any of this news gets out."

"But what about Lord Fitzroy?"

"What about him?" Cat said. "Just because I've found out I'm related to him doesn't mean that I have to stop living my own life, Bess."

"No, I suppose it doesn't!" Bess smiled slowly. "Yes, this is a wonderful idea. Do you know the tides?"

Cat nodded. "Of course! We can leave on the high tide just before midnight. I'll go now and prepare the crew. Don't be late!"

Bess hugged her and said, "Thanks, Cat; you always know what to do."

Rushing home, Bess wrote a note for her father and left it on his desk in the study. She didn't want to see him face-to-face, as he was still displeased with her. Perhaps time away would mellow his frustration.

So for all intents and purposes, he would now think she was staying with her elderly aunt in Kent again.

Two days later

Bess stood on the deck of *the Blue Belle* as she sailed gracefully through the waves. She breathed in the salty, fresh air and feasted her eyes on the vast expanse of the ocean, feeling her whole body relax. This was exactly what she had needed.

The wind blew her hair softly, carrying away her worries and replacing them with a newfound sense of liberation. They had been at sea for two days, and already her life on land seemed like a distant memory.

So what if Lord Fairchild sought to defame her character? Let him do his best! On her return, she would laugh off any mention of such a scandal and would somehow manage to turn the tables so the onus was on him.

But although she said the words, she knew it was just bravado and that, in reality, it wouldn't be that easy. At least out at sea, she could push those thoughts aside for now. A brief respite in a world of societal games.

She sensed movement next to her and turned to find Cat by her side. "Isn't it beautiful, Cat?"

Cat placed her hands on the railing and nodded. "Amazing. I will never tire of it."

As *the Blue Belle* continued its course, another ship emerged on the horizon, its sails billowing in the wind. "Ship ho!" The watchman said. He was high up in the crow's nest, his eyes peeled for any activity.

"A merchant ship, Pike?" Bess called up, hope in her voice.

"I can't make it out yet; it's too far away," he said.

Cat looked at her and said quickly, "I'll prepare the crew, just in case. If it's a Navy ship, we'll have to skedaddle!"

As Cat set about informing the big red-bearded McGregor and then the rest of the crew, Bess brought out her spyglass and raised it to the horizon, scanning along until her eyes fell on the other ship. It looked to be a similar size. She just hoped it was a heavily laden merchant ship rather than a naval vessel.

She lowered the spyglass for a moment and listened to the crew. They were lively, preparing for any outcome, and Bess could feel the adrenaline begin to pump through her slender body as she too waited to see which path they would take.

Raising the spyglass again, she located the ship, and then her heart skipped a beat as she recognised the familiar vessel. It was none other than Bill's ship, *the Avalon*, making its way towards them.

"Oh, Lord!" She murmured.

Memories of that fateful night over two weeks ago, when Bill had stood her up, flooded her mind, and a wave of anger washed over her. How could he have abandoned her without an explanation? The wound of that perceived betrayal still lingered, and her hand settled on the hilt of her cutlass angrily.

Cat appeared by her side. "Is that who I think it is?" She breathed, her eyes wide.

"Yes!" Bess hissed. "And I mean to show him who has the upper hand!"

"You're not going to attack his ship, are you?" Cat gasped.

"No, just him!" Bess spat angrily, her eyes fixed on the tall figure standing majestically at the helm. They were so close now that she needed no spyglass to recognise his fine figure.

As *the Avalon* drew nearer, Bess's frustration grew. She wanted to run away and leave Cat to deal with the rogue, but she also wanted satisfaction.

She confronted Bill the moment their ship came alongside, her voice laced with anger and hurt. "So you finally decided to show up, did you?"

"Is that any way to greet me?" He smiled, showing his even white teeth against his tanned skin. Bess almost swooned and then stopped herself. What was she thinking? Stand firm!

"Permission to come aboard, Captain," Bill called across.

"Permission denied!" Bess spat, planting her feet apart and her hands on her hips defiantly.

Bill tilted his head and raised an eyebrow. "So, this is how you want to play it, is it? I see."

Before she could fathom what he was doing, he had grabbed a rope and swung straight across. He landed in front of her and slipped his arm around her waist.

The crew went to intervene, but Cat raised a hand, stopping them instantly. She looked at the pair of them and then said to Bill, "What do you intend to do, Captain Bill?"

His eyes crinkled with mirth. "Bess and I have some unfinished business, so we can either discuss it here or on my ship." He turned his gaze back to Bess. "What's it to be, my sweet Bess?"

Bill looked into her green eyes, now blazing with anger. She looked even more beautiful than the last time they'd met. He could also see she was struggling with her emotions.

"Bess?" Cat prompted her. "What do you want us to do?"

He knew instantly the moment she capitulated when her body relaxed into his.

"I'll go with him." Bess said to Cat. "But know this, Bill, if you fail to return me, my crew will attack your ship in an instant!"

"Of course." He grinned, not at all intimidated by her threat.

Her lips tightened and her eyes narrowed, but before she could change her mind, he threw her over his shoulder, stood on the railing, and swung straight back over to *the Avalon*.

Chapter Nine

Captain Bill eyed Bess from across his cabin, watching her pace up and down, her vexation apparent. Even in her fury, she was breathtakingly beautiful. Her dark hair hung in waves down her back, and her green eyes sparkled like fine-cut gemstones.

She stopped and glared at him. "So, after leaving me waiting that night without a word, you expect me to believe your excuses now?" Her voice was filled with indignation, and her lips were tight with anger.

Bill tapped his fingers on the desk. She was so damn stubborn! "Bess, I'll say it again; I never stood you up. We had to escape the customs men, and then I was wounded and unable to leave my ship. Why won't you believe me when I say that I wanted nothing more than to be by your side that night?"

But Bess seemed too angry to listen. "You would say anything to absolve yourself!"

"Are you going to listen to anything I have to say?" He was starting to get angry himself now.

"No!"

He watched as her hand settled on the hilt of her cutlass. Was she seriously going to try and use that on him? His eyes shot to hers, and he saw that the thought had indeed crossed her mind.

His eyelids lowered, and his hand began to twitch. If she carried on, he knew one good way of making her calm down. He gave it one last shot.

"Why would I waste my breath lying to you? Have you thought about that?"

She rounded on him. "You're only covering your tracks because you have no other choice," she sneered. "You would have quite happily never seen me again. It's only because you came across my ship that you seek to hoodwink me."

"Hoodwink you?" He stood up and walked around the desk towards her. "I have no need to hoodwink anyone, my little firebrand. I have only spoken the plain truth, and if you cannot accept that, then that's your problem."

"Oh, go to hell!" She spat and spun on her heel, heading for the door. But Bill intercepted her in a heartbeat, his large hand settling on the wood and blocking her exit.

She looked up at him, her eyes spitting fire. "Get out of the way!"

"Or?" He asked, leaning his face closer to hers. He saw a moment of disconcertion before she cursed loudly and kicked him in the shins. Luckily, his boot took the impact, but the mere fact that she'd done it was the last straw.

Grabbing her wrist, he drew her away from the door and towards the desk.

She struggled like fury. "Get off me, you great big oaf! You lying, cheating bastard!"

He stopped for a moment and looked down at her, his eyes dark. "I should wash your mouth out with soap for those remarks!"

She scowled and went to kick him again, but he preempted her and simply swept her up into his arms. She pushed against his chest, but she was no match for his immense strength, and he soon had her positioned face down over his knee as he took a seat on one of the chairs.

Her pert little bottom, wrapped so prettily in black breeches, was just asking to be spanked, and her attitude truly deserved it. Without hesitation, he brought his hand swinging down onto her bottom, and the cabin was soon filled with the sounds of her wails and the ringing slaps that ensued. One after the other.

He kept her firmly in place by wrapping his muscular arm around her waist, so she had no chance to escape. Even though she did her best to struggle, she didn't budge. He meant for her to receive a sizzling backside in the hope it would calm her temper. And boy, what a temper she had!

Bess was madder than hell but also in a great deal of pain. Lord, his hands were huge! She should have known he'd be too eager to throw his weight around. Bastard! And worst of all, he seemed to be getting pleasure from it.

She winced as another harsh smack impacted her tender backside, and she kicked her legs up in the air. But nothing would stop the big brute from his quest.

She could feel her bottom begin to sizzle, and she just knew she wasn't going to be sitting comfortably later. A little too late, she realised that perhaps she should have just shut her mouth. But she had been too angry with him to keep quiet, and if she was honest, she was too damn upset. She really thought they had something between them, but the harsh reality was that she was just another conquest.

A tear slipped down her face, not only from her punishment but also from the realisation that she felt she'd been used and discarded. She hadn't admitted to herself how much it had hurt her until now.

A sob broke loose from her lips, and Bill's hand immediately stilled. She felt his grip relax, and the next thing, he was cradling her against his chest, his huge arms holding her close against his broad chest. For a moment, he didn't say anything and let her softly cry.

He smelled lovely. A mixture of leather and sea salt. Fresh and exciting. Despite the spanking, she felt safe in his arms, as though she belonged to him. Pulling back a bit, she looked up at him, and their eyes met.

Had she overreacted? Was he sincere? She so wanted to believe him.

He lifted his hand and touched her jaw, placing his thumb on her bottom lip. Her eyes shimmered with her recent tears, and her lips trembled at his touch.

When his mouth touched hers, gently at first, she responded willingly, her desire for him something she couldn't deny. He deepened the kiss, his tongue seeking entry to her warm and desirable depths.

Her heart soared. Even if he was the rogue she believed him to be, could she deny herself this pleasure? She wanted it just as much as he did. Two lovers lost in a moment in time.

His effect on her was electric, and she wanted him. It was that simple. She felt him lift her as he stood, and in two strides, they were on the four-poster bed. He didn't break the kiss for a second, and neither did she want him to. His lips were driving her crazy with desire.

She felt his hands on her breeches, and soon they were thrown to the floor. When his large hands cupped her sensitive bottom and his hot tongue seared her womanhood, she almost climaxed on the spot. The feeling was exquisite. He began a steady assault, his tongue working magic over her silken folds and her small nub of desire. Just when she thought she could take no more, her body tightened, and she lost herself in the myriad of stars that enveloped her.

Bill heard her cries of pleasure as they spilled from her voluptuous lips and quickly released his hard shaft from the confines of his breeches. Positioning himself at her entrance, he slid inside her soft, warm body as though they were made for each other.

He groaned with satisfaction and looked down at his sweet Bess, her face still contorted in the throes of passion. Good God, she was perfection itself. Leaning over her, he began to pump his hips steadily, noticing the way she moved in time with him. Her slender legs wrapped around his back as she pulled him in deeper, her small hands gripping his forearms.

"Oh, Bill!"

"Yes, my sweet Bess?" He nuzzled her neck, drinking in her heady perfume.

"Can't we stay like this forever?" She whispered, her voice honey soft with yearning.

"I have no objection. In fact..." In one swift move, he rolled over, so she was on top of him. "I think we should stay like *this* forever."

He noted the look of surprise on Bess's face, but when he placed his hands on her bottom and thrust upwards, she soon began to move in rhythm. Throwing her head back, she gasped with unabashed pleasure.

If there was one thing he was learning about Bess, it was that she possessed not only a fiery nature but also a passionate one, and the combination made their encounters beyond compare.

Reaching up, he pulled down her blouse and cupped one of her plump breasts. The nipple was already hard and pink; her arousal evident. She let out a small sigh, and bringing her head forward, her green eyes settled on him.

"Bess, you are so beautiful." He murmured.

He thrust inside her at the same time and had the satisfaction of seeing her eyes close and her mouth open with a small gasp of delight.

Pumping harder, he quickly took her over the edge, and as her body clamped around his member, he rolled over again, so she was beneath him. With a few hard thrusts, he gave in to the heady throes of passion and withdrew at the last minute as he climaxed.

If there was one thing in life that Bill had learned from others, it was never to get a woman pregnant out of wedlock.

Rising up, he took Bess in his arms and gave her a lingering kiss. "You look like the cat that got the cream," he remarked, smiling.

She stretched and almost purred back, "Well, it does feel a little like that."

He trailed a finger over her soft lips, down her neck, and over the swell of her breasts. She closed her eyes and sighed softly before opening them again and fixing him with a look.

"Were you speaking the truth earlier when you said you got wounded?" She asked.

For an answer, he lifted his leg and, lowering his breeches further, pointed at the three-inch-long scar on his thigh. It was still a little red in places, but nothing that wouldn't fade in time, although he would always have a visible scar of sorts.

"Oh!" she exclaimed.

"You see. I only told you the truth."

"I'm sorry I distrusted you." Bess said in a small voice.

He lifted her hand and kissed her knuckles. "Now, perhaps this is the time to tell you about my double life, and then you can reveal yours."

She smiled. "Very well."

A little while later, they both lay in silence, side by side, after having bared their souls to one another.

"So you took to a life of piracy because you were looking for adventure?" He remarked, raising an eyebrow. "Well, you certainly got that, didn't you?"

Bess shot him a wicked smile. "Indeed, I did. Especially when I met a rather overbearing pirate captain."

He growled and nuzzled her neck, making her squeal while his large hand cupped her still sizzling, plump little bottom. "So, my little firebrand, what do you intend to do now?" Bill asked her, grazing her neck with his teeth. "Will you marry Lord Fairchild?"

There was a pause before she answered. "In all truth, I have already told him that I don't wish to marry him."

He raised himself up. "You have? How did he react? I cannot see someone like Lord Fairchild taking such a rejection without retaliation."

"In that, you are correct." Bess said despondently. "That's why Cat and I are at sea. Lord Fairchild had someone spy on me, and he reported that he had seen you and me in the stables together. He has threatened to ruin my family name because of it."

Bess watched Bill's face grow dark with anger. "I always knew he was a weak man, but he is also a coward. What man would seek to cause such a scandal?" He said.

"Are you worried about your name being involved with mine?" she asked.

"Not at all. I am just aggrieved that he has put you in such a position. What did your father have to say?"

Bess looked a little sheepish. "Well, in all truth, I didn't tell him about Lord Fairchild's threats. I just left home." When Bill shot her a disapproving look, she quickly reassured him. "I did leave him a note. He thinks I am staying with an elderly relative."

"Well, that's something." He went quiet for a moment and appeared to be deep in thought. "I have a solution, but one that you might not wish to do."

"Oh?"

"Marry me."

"Pardon?"

"Marry me!" He said it again. "It's the perfect solution."

Chapter Ten

Bess could hardly believe she was hearing correctly, but looking into Bill's eyes, she could see the sincerity.

Bill took a deep breath, his voice steady but filled with a sense of urgency. "Lord Fairchild's threats against you are real, Bess. He saw us enter the stables that night, and now, because you have refused to marry him, he plans to defame your character. But if we were to marry, it would provide us with a cover story and a shield against his accusations. It would protect your reputation."

Bess's brows furrowed in contemplation. Marrying Bill would certainly stop any further gossip, but the idea of a strategic marriage seemed rather daunting, to say the least.

She held Bill's gaze and said, "But what would you get out of such a marriage?"

"You, my sweet Bess. Nothing more, nothing less. I admire you in so many ways, and I don't want to see your name tarnished by a weak, unpleasant rogue like Lord Fairchild." He stroked her thigh. "Think about it logically. We are both captains of ships that plunder and steal from others. We understand each other. So let's get married."

"But where would we live?"

"We'll buy a house near your own. I've heard Lumley Hall is up for sale. I have accumulated a good deal of money from my exploits, Bess, and I expect you have too. We can set up a life there together for outward appearances, but both lead our lives at sea as we wish."

Bill's voice grew softer. "I know this proposal may have arisen from necessity, but it is with all sincerity that I ask. I care about you, Bess, and together we can face Lord Fairchild's threats. He will rue the day he threatened you."

Bess took a moment to absorb Bill's words, her heart torn between caution and the yearning for a future where she had no worry about any sort of scandal. But she had always thought of marrying for love, and although she knew she desired Bill, was that akin to love?

Did he love her? Did it matter?

Accepting his proposal would require courage, but the alternative was a life tainted by scandal and injustice. The very idea was abhorrent.

With a gentle smile, Bess reached for Bill's hand, intertwining their fingers. "You're right, Bill. It will certainly solve many problems, and I do love life at sea. I would miss it if I had to marry someone like Lord Fairchild."

Bill's face lit up. "I told you it would be a good idea." He pulled Bess into his embrace, kissing her fiercely. "Besides, we get to make love whenever we like and wherever we like."

"Now that, my handsome captain, is something I heartily agree with!"

They were soon lost in each other's arms, and they knew that their decision to marry was not just a means of protection but a declaration of their commitment to one another.

As for love, maybe that would come in time, and at the moment, that would suffice.

As *the Avalon* sailed away, Bess's gaze lingered on the handsome captain. He was standing proudly at the helm, his tricorn hat perched neatly on his head and his arms folded across his massive chest.

They'd agreed to meet up two weeks later, where Bill, under his title as Lord Maidstone, would ask her father for her hand in marriage.

Bess was nervous about the whole thing. She hoped her father wouldn't refuse. There was no reason to do so, but then her father was as stubborn as she was. He would interrogate Bill; that was for certain. But Bill could charm the birds from the trees, so she was quietly confident it would go ahead.

Cat sidled up to her. "I still can't believe what's happened."

"Me neither, but it makes perfect sense."

"I suppose it does," Cat sniggered. "I would love to see the look on Lord Fairchild's face when he finds out who you'll be marrying! That'll wipe the smile off his arrogant face."

"Hopefully I'll never see him again. That was a close call. I'm so glad I never married him." She shuddered at the very thought.

"Well then," Cat said, rubbing her hands together. "I think we should go to the cabin and have a glass of that special wine we pilfered to celebrate!"

"What a splendid idea!" Bess grinned, and linking her arm through Cat's, they walked towards the cabin.

McGregor watched them go and smiled. They were a feisty pair of lasses, and he couldn't help but admire them. One fair, one dark, but both as charismatic as the other.

Looking up at the crow's nest, he called up, "Take a break, Pike. I'll keep look out for now." And taking out his clay pipe, he leaned on the railing and leisurely began to fill it with tobacco as he watched the sun dip below the horizon.

Two weeks later

Bess and Cat sailed into the familiar cove at Portsmouth, their ship laden with the spoils of their encounters with not one but two merchant ships during their time at sea.

The crew was more than happy, and McGregor would now sail *the Blue Belle* to Cornwall, where he would sell their wares. The money would be shared equally between all of them. It was only fair.

As Bess stepped out of the tender onto the beach, she thanked Griffin, the coxswain, and as soon as Cat joined her, he rowed back to the ship.

"Oh, I confess to being quite excited to be home this time." Cat declared. "I'm looking forward to visiting with Lord Fitzroy again."

Bess looked at her dressed in her fine clothes, a far cry from their usual appearance on board ship, wearing breeches and bandanas. They had both changed into their finest dresses as soon as *the Blue Belle* had sailed into the cove. It wouldn't do for anyone they knew to see them dressed as pirates. Now there truly would be a scandal!

Lifting the hem of her skirt and holding her carpet bag tightly, Bess began crossing the fine sandy beach, following Cat as she climbed the stone steps up the small cliff. It was their usual route home, and it was always very quiet.

Bess was just as excited to return home, for she knew that she would be seeing Bill any day. For a moment, she felt a bit anxious. What if he didn't turn up? What if he had lied again?

She shook her head. No, he had been sincere.

She knew that facing her father and the consequences of her absence would be a challenge she could not avoid. What if Lord Fairchild had already begun his devious attack on her character?

Reaching the streets of Portsmouth, Bess and Cat made their way to the inn, where they hoped to hire a carriage for Bess to take her home. Cat was staying at the tavern, which was within walking distance, but not so for Bess.

They were just about to go inside when Adam stepped out. They were all as surprised as each other, but then Adam exclaimed, with a hint of annoyance in his voice, "Elizabeth, where have you been? Father has been worried sick. You said you were visiting our aunt in Kent, but I went to see her, and she told me you hadn't been there for months."

Bess's heart sank. Oh lord! This was all she needed.

Cat immediately came to her aid. "Oh, it's my fault, Adam."

He turned his gaze on her, and his eyes narrowed suspiciously. "What do you mean?"

"I asked Bess to come and stay with me for a while because she was upset over cutting off her engagement with Lord Fairchild."

He rounded on his sister. "So why lie and say you were in Kent? Something isn't right here."

"We're not hiding anything, Adam." Bess said, "I only told Father I was in Kent because I didn't want to be disturbed. I wanted time alone."

"You weren't on your own." He accused her. "You were with Cat."

"Well, you know what I mean."

"Hmmmm."

She licked her lips nervously and tried to distract him. "What did you go all the way to Kent for anyway? What was so urgent?"

She had a feeling she knew, but she had to be sure.

"Lord Fairchild has been causing a ruckus by saying you were caught with Lord Maidstone in the stables. Lord Maidstone of all people. You don't even know the man properly!"

"Well, no...!"

"I have already dealt with him myself for daring to even mention such a thing!"

Cat's eyes widened. "What did you do?"

"Gave him a right-hander."

Both Bess and Cat clapped hands to their mouths and looked at each other.

"Good lord!" Cat breathed.

"Oh, my!" Bess said, wondering if this was going to cause any ructions for Bill's meeting with her father.

Taking a deep breath, Bess met Adam's gaze and began to explain, "Adam, I... I didn't mean for things to turn out this way. But, you see, Lord Maidstone and I want to get married."

Adam was even more surprised than before. "Lord Maidstone? How did this happen?"

"It's a long story, but, suffice to say, he has asked for my hand in marriage, and I consented. He's coming to visit our father any day now."

Adam went quiet, staring at her with a bewildered expression. "To say I'm confused would be an understatement."

Cat placed her hand on his arm and said, "Truly, Adam, I would just accept it. Some things are better left unsaid."

Her remark seemed to alleviate his worries a little, and turning to Bess, he said, "You were always a willful little madam, so I guess this should come as no surprise."

"Not always!" Bess objected.

"Always!" he noted, shooting her a look, daring her to disagree. She hushed her mouth and pouted, deciding not to push the issue.

"Perhaps you should return home together." Cat suggested. "We were here to hire a carriage."

"I have one already waiting." Adam said to her, and then, his expression softening, he said, "May I call upon you this week, Cat?"

She blushed a little and said, "Of course, I would like that."

His gaze lingered a little, something Bess noticed immediately. Oh yes, her brother liked Cat; that was certain.

"Come, sister." Adam said firmly, "We'd better return home so you can calm our father down. He is worried beyond reason."

As her brother turned his back, Bess squeezed Cat's hand and whispered, "Thank you!"

With a friend like Cat around, she would always be fine!

Two days later

Bess anxiously awaited the arrival of Captain Bill, or, should she say, Lord Maidstone, at her home. He'd sent a message to say he would be coming this afternoon, and Bess had been staring up the drive since just after lunch.

To say she was nervous would be an understatement.

Her father had been mightily relieved to see her arrive back home and seemed somewhat placated when she explained she had stayed with her friend, Cat. He still admonished her for lying about going to Kent and told her it must never happen again.

When she informed him about Lord Maidstone's marriage proposal, he was just as surprised as Adam. He had heard the rumours of her indiscretion with Lord Maidstone but had dismissed them immediately. But now that he knew she wanted to marry the nobleman, he wasn't so sure.

Bess had opted to reveal that they had been outside near the stables and that Lord Maidstone had only kissed her hand, nothing else. The rest was just Lord Fairchild's wicked attempt to blacken her name because he had been usurped.

So after a lot of persuasion, her father agreed to meet with Lord Maidstone and see what he had to say for himself. Only then, and if he deemed it fitting, would he give his consent.

Bess spied Bill as soon as he entered the drive. He was sitting upon a jet-black stallion, and his attire was every bit the gentleman. No one would have believed that he could be a pirate captain!

Bess's heart raced with anticipation, her eyes gleaming with nervous excitement. Oh, how could her father possibly deny a marriage to such a man? Quickly, she headed downstairs to greet her intended.

Bill dismounted by the front steps and was immediately greeted by Bess. She looked stunningly beautiful, and when their eyes met, they locked in a silent understanding of the commitment they were going to make together.

He wanted to sweep her up in his arms and kiss her fiercely but knew that decorum forbade it, and with eyes watching from the house, he had to act with due respect. He resigned himself to a lingering kiss on her knuckles. It brought a bloom of pink to her cheeks, and he could tell by the rapid rise and fall of her bosom that she desired much more.

With a twinkle in his eye, he said, "Miss Warren, may I declare how beautiful you look this morning?"

She smiled prettily and said, "Why, thank you, Lord Maidstone, and may I return the compliment? You look quite resplendent, if I may say so."

Bill leaned nearer to her and whispered in her ear, "And how I would like to make love to you right this very second."

She giggled and drew her bottom lip in with her small white teeth. "Why, my Lord, how presumptuous of you!"

"Little madam." He growled low, smiling.

Bess linked her arm through Bill's and led him up the stone staircase into the large hallway. "My father is waiting for you in the study."

Reaching the wooden door, she knocked on the door. "Papa, Lord Maidstone is here to see you."

"Come in," he answered, his voice a little clipped. But that was nothing unusual with her father. Even so, she couldn't help but still feel nervous.

She squeezed Bill's hand and stood aside as Bill, carrying his usual air of confidence, approached her father. The door closed, and Bess stood there for a moment, pondering whether to eavesdrop, but a quiet cough nearby from the butler told her it would only be reported. So, a little defeated, she wandered outside to the terrace and resigned herself to a long wait.

A good half hour later, just when Bess thought she could take no more, Bill finally appeared.

She rushed up to him and said, "Well? What did he say? Did he say yes?"

Bill raised an eyebrow and sighed, his face grim. "Can we go somewhere quiet?"

Her eyes widened, and she felt a jolt of dismay rip through her. Had her father denied his request? Oh, lord. "We can go into the rose gardens. No one will disturb us there."

She led him along the gravel path, around the back of the house, and into the secluded rose garden. It was a beautiful place to be, but today she saw none of its beauty; her mind focused on only one thing: Bill.

As soon as they were in private, she turned around and looked at him. "What happened?"

"I'm sorry, Bess, but he... I don't know how to say this, but... he said yes!"

For a moment, she just blinked at him, wondering if she'd heard him correctly, but when he gave his usual devilish grin, she pursed her lips. "Oh, upon my word, you are annoying!"

She slapped his arm, and he grabbed her hand before she could pull back. "Now, my naughty Bess, is that any way to behave?" He drew her against him and kissed her soundly before saying, "You know what happens to naughty girls when they misbehave, don't you?" His eyes glinted with intent, and Bess's eyes widened.

"Don't you dare!" She breathed, trying to pull back, but Bill had other ideas.

Quickly throwing her over his lap, he threw up her dress and landed three quick swats in succession on her delectable bottom, admiring the way the plump little cheeks jiggled under his hand. "Ah, my fine Bess, just think; I'll be able to do this as often as I like when we're married."

She struggled to rise off his lap, but he kept her firmly in place with just one large hand, so she huffed loudly and said, "If you think that by marrying me, you can do this anytime, then you are mistaken."

Despite her words, she couldn't help but feel the thrill of desire that shot through her. Marrying Captain Bill was certainly going to be a challenge, but an exciting one!

Chapter Eleven

The familiar doors of the tavern swung open as Bess stepped inside, and she looked around for Cat. They had arranged to meet up to talk about their recent news. It had only been a few days, but they both had tales to tell.

Bess wanted to share the news of her father's agreement to her marriage with Bill, and she was excited to hear how Cat was getting along with Lord Fitzroy.

Spotting Cat at a table in the corner, Bess made her way through the bustling crowd, her eyes lighting up as she joined her.

Cat grinned at her happily. "Bess, I've been dying to know what's going on. Sit down and tell me everything!"

She poured her a glass of wine and pushed it towards her. Bess took a satisfying mouthful before answering. "Father agreed to our marriage. Bill looked so fine, Cat. You wouldn't believe it was the same swaggering pirate that leads *the Avalon*." She sniggered. "Oh dear, if only my father knew!"

Cat's eyes widened. "Well, let's hope that never happens!"

"And how about you? Have you been to visit your grandfather?"

"It sounds odd to call Lord Fitzroy my grandfather. But that's what he is." She laughed softly before continuing. "Well, I did go to see him, and he wants me to go and live at Woodleigh Manor. But I'm not so sure. What do you think?"

Bess pondered her words. "Well, as you are the heiress, then there seems to be no point in you not moving in. It would certainly be a change for you."

"But will it hinder me from sailing on *the Blue Belle?* I shouldn't like to give my life of piracy up, Bess." She worried her bottom lip. "When you marry, Bill, you'll still be able to do as you like, won't you?"

"Yes, we have both agreed that our lives won't change in that aspect. So you and I can carry on our escapades."

Bess's own excitement wavered for a moment as she wondered what Cat should do.

She understood the conflicting emotions that she must be experiencing, torn between the allure of a life of luxury and the freedom of the open seas. Could she do both? Would Lord Fitzroy have too many expectations of her?

Bess reached across the table, her hand gently touching Cat's. "I don't quite know what to suggest, Cat," Bess said, her voice filled with empathy. "Life on the sea has always been our escape, our source of fun and adventure. It's more exciting than I care to admit, but life is also full of choices. I guess you have to decide what matters most to you."

Cat sighed, her gaze fixed on their intertwined hands. "Bess, I love the sea so much, you know I do, and I love the thrill of our adventures together. But Lord Fitzroy's offer presents a life of security and comfort that I haven't had since my adoptive parents died. But I fear that if I choose that path, I may lose the freedom to sail the high seas."

Bess nodded, understanding Cat's dilemma. "I think I would go and live there and see how things progress. If Lord Fitzroy truly cares for you, he won't try to control you. If he does, you must put your foot down. I know you can't tell him about our secret life, so come up with an excuse for your absence when needed. Like I did."

Cat's eyes brightened. "You're right, Bess. It would be foolish of me not to move in, but I need to clarify that I want my own space. I won't let him control me, that's for sure."

Bess smiled and said, "I have faith in you, Cat. Your strength and determination have always been your greatest assets. I've seen you battle against all manner of men, so I am certain Lord Fitzroy will be an easy conquest should he even attempt to curb your nature," she laughed. "I think he'll soon find out that you have a fiery temper and maybe even find himself at the end of your cutlass!"

"Now that would shock him!"

"Talking of *the Blue Belle* – can you meet the crew next week and tell them to return in September? My wedding is in a few weeks, and I want to enjoy some time with Bill before setting sail again."

Cat laughed and raised her glass. "I will do that with pleasure. To you and me, Bess, and our rosy futures!"

Bess clinked her glass against Cat's, and they downed the wine in one go. "You know what we need?" Bess winked at her. "A fine glass of rum!"

"Amen to that!"

Within a month, Miss Elizabeth Warren and Lord William Maidstone became husband and wife. They had opted for a small wedding with only close relatives and friends present. It suited them better that way.

At the end of the reception, and with well wishes showered upon them, they stepped into the carriage and made their way to Lumley Hall, their new home.

They'd grown even closer over the last few weeks, and Bess had seen a different side to him. He was as commanding in his title of Lord Maidstone as he was as Captain Bill – his voice thundering and bellowing out orders to the tradesmen as they quickly went about updating Lumley Hall. They scurried about, just as lively as the crew on *the Avalon*, transforming the house with the best fabrics and furnishings that his plundered treasures could buy.

The house had been finished in record time, and she sensed a look of relief on the tradesmen's faces as they packed up their bags and left.

The thought made her smile, and Bill eyed her from across the interior of the carriage. "What are you smiling about, might I ask?"

"You." Bess replied simply.

"Oh?" He moved across to sit beside her. "And why, pray tell, do I make you smile?" His eyes glinted with menace, and Bess's mouth twitched with mirth.

"Don't think to threaten me, Captain Bill!"

"You're all mine now, my sweet Bess, and you should know by now that I don't just threaten; I act!"

In one swift move, he had her face down over his lap, and Bess giggled. "Why, Captain Bill, whatever are you doing?"

He lifted her skirts and ran his hand over her plump little buttocks. "Just admiring your beautiful derriere, my love."

She closed her eyes, thrilling at his touch. "Can't you wait until we get home?"

"Not really, no." His hand slipped beneath the parting in her bloomers, and he sank a finger between her silken folds. "It looks like you cannot wait either, my little temptress."

Bess couldn't deny it and parted her thighs to allow him easier access. Laughing softly, he set about bringing her to orgasm, plying his finger over her sensitive little nub again and again until, with a small cry, she reached a fiery climax.

Lifting her up, he sat her on his lap facing him, so her knees were either side of his, and she felt his stiff shaft at her entrance. Her eyes widened, but before she could say anything, his lips captured hers in a fiery kiss.

He pushed up into her willing body, his hands holding her hips and guiding her body as he plundered her depths. The rhythm of the carriage seemed to enhance the experience, and it wasn't long before Bess was nearing another orgasm.

He moved his mouth from her lips, and releasing one of her breasts from their confines, he fastened over one pink nipple. "Oh!" She gasped. The feeling of his hot tongue quickly sent her over the edge.

He thrust harder as she contracted around his manhood, and, keeping a steady rhythm, he reached his own pinnacle, his gasp of pleasure evident.

Bess collapsed against him, burying her head against his neck and inhaling his intoxicating masculine scent.

"I don't care if you don't love me, Bill, but I love you." She murmured.

He went still for a moment and, gently pulling her away, looked deep into her striking green eyes. "What makes you think I don't love you?"

"You've never said it," Bess said quietly. "And I know this marriage is only for convenience."

"My sweet Bess, I am a man of few words, but I can tell you now that you have my undying devotion. I love you more than life itself."

"You do?"

He nodded. "I've known it for a while, but I wasn't sure you returned my feelings." He kissed her. "But now I know."

Her eyes sparkled with love. "Then we can start our new life in Lumley Hall the way it should be." She frowned for a moment and asked him, "You didn't withdraw just now, like you usually do."

He shook his head. "No, we are man and wife in the eyes of God, and if he wills a babe upon us, then it is our fate, my love."

She smiled and snuggled into his chest, happy and content that marrying Bill was the best decision she had ever made.

Two months later

Bess stood at the helm of *the Blue Belle*, the wind tousling her hair and the salty scent of the sea filling her senses. Cat was by her side, her face alert and her body taut, as they came alongside the merchant ship, *the Margarette*.

Out of the corner of her eye, Bess could see *the Avalon* bearing down upon them, but she ignored it. First come, first served, as far as she was concerned, plus she could almost taste the sweet smell of victory.

"McGregor, prepare to board!" Bess called over to him, her voice tinged with excitement.

"Are you sure you want to do this?" Cat cautioned her. "You do know *the Avalon* is right behind us?"

"Of course I want to do this! Our gain is his loss!" She laughed. "He should have been quicker!"

Her crew was ready and waiting. They had already fired their cannons, and the merchant captain had the obvious look of defeat on his face. Perhaps his paltry pay wasn't worth wasting his life for!

"I want the captain." Bess said to Cat, "You take the one next to him!"

Cat grinned. "I love a good fight!"

Throwing the grappling hooks over, the two captains and many of the crew clambered aboard.

Bess headed for the merchant captain, her cutlass raised and ready. He withdrew his own and, looking extremely nervous, got ready to fight, but it never came to that.

Suddenly, Bess heard a voice right next to her. "What the devil are you doing?" It was Bill, and he was livid.

"I'm doing what you should be doing! Only you're too slow!" Bess hissed, still holding her cutlass against the very scared-looking captain.

"Alec!" Bill bellowed.

He appeared in an instant and said, "Yes, Captain?"

"Take this man and tie him up. Then empty the holds." He looked at Bess, his eyes glinting with anger. "Captain Bess is coming with me."

"Oh no, I'm not!"

She squealed loudly as she found herself quickly thrown over his shoulder, her cutlass clattering to the deck. She beat her fists against him and kicked her legs, but it was all to no avail.

The merchant captain watched in fascination while Alec tied his hands behind his back and couldn't help asking, "What on earth was that all about?"

Alec smirked. "Oh, just a man taming his wife."

"His wife?"

Alec laughed at the captain's expression, and before he could ask any more questions, he led him over to the main mast, where he neatly and expertly tied him to the post.

Bess's indignant cries diminished as Bill swung her across to his ship and disappeared inside his cabin. Alec knew it wouldn't be long before her shrieks from a blistered behind would be heard reverberating around the ship. If there was one thing he knew about his captain, it was that he didn't stand for insubordination—from anyone.

As the merchant ship was relieved of its vast quantities of goods and divided between the two pirate ships, Cat stood at the helm of her ship and glanced across at *the Avalon*.

She knew Bess would be back, sporting a very sore bottom but with a smile as broad as can be. Their clash of tempers was becoming legendary.

Would she ever experience such a marriage? A vision of Adam came to mind, and she smiled softly. Now there was a man she wouldn't mind spending her life with, but what would he think if he found out she was a pirate captain?

She breathed in a lungful of fresh sea air and shrugged to herself. She would leave her future to fate. For now, she was going to have a welcome glass of rum and wait for her partner in crime, for she knew that their lives would forever be entwined.

The end

CAPTIVE TO THE HEART
THE PIRATES QUEST BOOK II

Chapter One

The English Channel, 1820

The sun cast its golden rays across the vast expanse of the ocean as *the Blue Belle,* a formidable pirate ship, sailed steadily towards England's shores. Captain Cat stood at the helm next to McGregor, the quartermaster, watching as his weathered hands expertly guided the ship through the gentle swells. By her side was her best friend and fellow pirate captain, Bess, her gaze fixed on the horizon, her spyglass in hand.

For the past three weeks, Cat had been living her life as she usually did, sailing the open seas, chasing adventure, and revelling in the freedom that comes with it. Now, as their present trip neared its end, she couldn't help but feel a little excited.

For as soon as she returned home, she would be moving from her lodgings at the *Fisherman's Joy* tavern into the opulent home of her grandfather's grand estate, Woodleigh.

She had only recently been introduced to her grandfather, Lord Fitzroy, when he hired a lawyer to find her. His daughter had revealed to him on her deathbed that she had born a child out of wedlock many years ago and given the baby girl up for adoption.

After an investigation, it was proven that Cat was his granddaughter and the sole heir to Woodleigh Manor. And what a manor it was!

That had been a few months ago, and now, after a lot of deliberation, she was ready to move into her new home. Sort of. She still didn't know if she was doing the right thing, but she was willing to give it a go.

But to be truthful, the thing she was most nervous about was keeping her secret life hidden from Lord Fitzroy. He knew nothing of her escapades as a pirate captain, and for now, she intended to keep it that way.

She had been a pirate captain of *the Blue Belle* for several years, along with Bess, and one thing she never intended to give up was her life on the high seas. It was far too exciting!

She would never let her grandfather take that away from her, and she knew that he would be mortified if he realised what she did! In fact, he might even disown her.

What if she regretted moving to the big house, though? What if her grandfather decided to control her life? She hadn't known him long enough yet to fully know his character traits, but from what she had seen so far, he seemed stern but fair.

She was twenty-six years old, and since her adoptive parents died ten years ago, she had been in control of her own destiny. The thought of someone else telling her what to do didn't sit well with her at all.

So she was playing a dangerous game, but it was one she was willing to experience. Life was not all sugary sweet, and she was no milksop maid. She was Captain Cat. No man had put her down yet, and she would soon put her grandfather in his place if he sought to do so.

As *the Blue Belle* continued its course, a small merchant ship came into view. Its sails billowed in the wind, a stark contrast to the sleek and formidable appearance of Cat's pirate vessel. A mischievous glint danced in her eyes as she turned to Bess.

"Have we got room in the hold for a little more booty?" Cat asked, her voice brimming with mischief, and coyly twirling a strand of her long blonde hair around her finger.

Bess laughed, her eyes immediately lighting up with devilment. "I'm sure we can find room!"

McGregor, a red-bearded giant of a man, threw his head back and laughed. "That's what I like about you two. There's always room for more!"

With a swift command, Cat ordered McGregor to set a course to intercept the merchant vessel whilst Bess prepared the crew for action. The ship was alive with activity, and Cat could feel the adrenaline rush through her veins. This was what she loved and couldn't give up. It was far too exciting.

As the two ships drew closer, Cat raised her spyglass and spoke aloud. "She's a fine-looking ship. I reckon she should have a good amount of treasure in those holds of hers!" She moved the spyglass along the hull to find out its name. "*The Pandora*".

Moving the spyglass again, she couldn't help but notice the striking figure of the other captain, his strong physique and piercing gaze catching her attention. He was staring straight at her.

Bess had already noticed him. "Hmmm, that captain's quite a looker, isn't he?" she remarked, a playful smile tugging at the corners of her lips.

Cat sniggered. "Don't let Bill hear you say such a thing! You'll be straight over his knee!"

Bess was recently married to Captain Bill, owner and captain of the notorious pirate ship called *the Avalon*. He also led a dual life, and on land, he was known as Lord Maidstone. They had a loving, if not fiery, relationship.

Bess pulled a face. "Bill's not here to find out, so I, for one, am not going to worry about it." Her voice was tinged with amusement. "It'll be interesting to see if this captain's swordsmanship matches his handsome face."

"Let me at him! I saw him first," Cat declared.

As Bess was about to argue back, *the Pandora* launched the first cannon, and the skirmish began. The air filled with the roar of cannons and the clash of steel as *the Blue Belle's* crew swung across the divide, attacking the merchant vessel with zealous pursuit. Their manpower was far superior to *the Pandora's,* and it soon began to show.

Cat, her heart pounding with adrenaline, engaged in a fierce swordfight with the dashing captain of *the Pandora.* He was tall and lithe, his dark blonde hair tied back beneath his tricorn hat, and his sharp blue eyes full of anger.

Their blades danced in a display of skill and determination.

At first, he seemed surprised to see a female brandishing a sword and, in his limited knowledge, thought she would be an easy opponent, but he soon learned how wrong he could be.

With each parry and thrust, Cat's confidence soared. Her natural prowess in combat showed, and soon she had the advantage. However, amidst the excitement of the skirmish, Cat felt a sharp pain shoot through her forearm. The captain's blade had found its mark, leaving behind a shallow cut. She winced, and when she saw the triumphant smile he shot her, it only fuelled her desire to defeat the bastard even more.

Parrying even harder and more determined than ever, Cat, with a swift manoeuvre, finally managed to disarm the dashing captain and pin him down, her laughter echoing through the air and her sparkling blue eyes showing her wicked pleasure in his defeat.

He eyed her angrily, and with her blade at his throat, she leaned down and placed a kiss on his lips.

"Bravo, Captain; you fought well." She grinned wickedly into his face, enjoying her victorious moment. Looking around, she saw one of her crew members and shouted at him to tie the captain up.

Swinging back over to *the Blue Belle,* she immediately went below decks to see the ship's surgeon, Monroe.

"I wish you'd leave the fighting to the men, Captain," he tutted, showing his disapproval. "It's a dangerous game you're playing."

"I'm not playing at anything!" Cat snapped back at him. "Anyway, this is only a tiny cut, and I was the victor."

"I wouldn't call it tiny. Hold still; this might sting."

She winced as he put one of his ointments on it, and then he swiftly bound it up with a tight bandage.

"Leave that on for a couple of days. I'll come and take another look at it; don't go taking it off yourself. I know what you're like."

Cat rolled her eyes. "I only did it that one time!"

He lowered his glasses and looked over the rims at her. "Once is too many."

She pulled a face and departed his quarters, leaving him grumbling to himself.

Bess was on deck, helping organise the goods transfer between the ships. She frowned as she saw Cat's arm. "Oh, what happened to you?" Her eyes were wide as she lifted Cat's arm to peer closely at the bandage.

"The captain nicked his blade on my arm, but it's only a small cut. Besides, it was worth it to fight against him. I thoroughly enjoyed it. This will be my battle scar."

Bess tilted her head. "Are you truly alright?"

"Yes, Bess. Please don't worry. Now, tell me what bounty we have."

With *the Pandora's* goods now safely transferred onto *the Blue Belle,* Cat gave directions to Jasper, the first mate, to continue their journey towards England and their secret cove.

As the sun began its descent, casting a beautiful orange glow over the sea, Cat stood at the bow next to Bess.

"I love this time of night," she said softly.

"Me too," Bess agreed. "Everything seems so peaceful."

"Will Bill be back home before you?"

"He should be. I hope so anyway. I'm so looking forward to seeing him." She turned sideways and looked at Cat directly. "Are you still going through with your plan to move into Woodleigh?"

Cat nodded. "Yes, I'm going to see how it goes. Lord Fitzroy had better not try and tell me what to do, though! I won't stand for it."

McGregor appeared by their side, holding a large bottle of rum in one hand and three glasses in the other. He grinned and held it up to them.

"I thought we should try a bit of this. *The Pandora's* captain was mightily annoyed that I nabbed it, so it must be a good 'un."

"We won't say no, will we, Bess?" Cat laughed.

"No, we damn well won't!" Bess agreed.

As the sun dipped below the horizon, the three of them clinked glasses and drained the contents of the rum. As suspected, it tasted like nectar, and before long, Cat and Bess were treated to McGregor's deep vocals as he attempted to sing a shanty. It was terrible, and Cat looked at Bess with tears of laughter in her eyes. Oh, yes. She could never give this life up. It was far too much fun.

Woodleigh Manor

A few days after docking, Cat stood at the entrance of Woodleigh Manor, nervously clasping her hands together. She had arrived at her grandfather's vast mansion to begin this new part of her life, but she still wasn't certain if it was the right thing to do.

She worried her bottom lip and looked up at the grandeur of the opulent mansion. The size of it literally took her breath away, and to think that she was heiress to such a grand house! She still found it hard to believe.

Taking a deep breath, she trod the steps to the front entrance. As the heavy wooden doors swung open, she stepped inside, trying to quell her nerves. She was greeted by the housekeeper, Mrs Hargrove, a stern but kind woman who had been with Lord Fitzroy for years. Cat had met her before and had immediately taken to her.

"Welcome to Woodleigh Manor, Miss Penley," Mrs Hargrove said with a warm smile. "Lord Fitzroy has been eagerly awaiting your arrival."

"Oh, I hope I haven't kept him waiting."

"No, he's happily occupied in the drawing room at the moment."

"My luggage is at the bottom of the steps. Can you arrange for it to be put in my room, please?" Cat said, smiling.

"Certainly, Miss. Now, if you'll follow me, I'll take you to him."

Cat followed Mrs Hargrove through the large hall, adorned with intricate tapestries and elegant chandeliers. Everything was very tastefully decorated, and she couldn't wait to show Bess everything when she came to visit.

As they entered the drawing room, Cat's eyes immediately landed on a pair of captivating green eyes that met her gaze from across the room.

It was Adam Warren, Bess's brother, a man she'd secretly admired for a while now. He was the lawyer who had revealed her connection to Lord Fitzroy, so it was only fitting that he was here now, although his presence was a little unexpected.

She smiled at him, and she couldn't help but feel a flutter of excitement. He had an air of authority about him, but he wasn't an arrogant man—quite the opposite. He was dressed smartly as always, and his dark, wavy hair was swept back fashionably. He was so handsome.

He was also oblivious to the fact that she and his sister were pirates, and it was best it remained that way. He would most probably have a fit if he knew!

Lord Fitzroy turned around and greeted her warmly. "Catherine, welcome, my dear, welcome. Adam has only recently arrived himself." He swept his hand out. "Take a seat, do. I've already ordered some refreshments."

Lord Fitzroy was a fine-looking man with grey hair and the same blue eyes that Cat possessed.

Cat settled onto the end of a comfortable couch and tried to relax, but it was hard. She was only used to living in the tavern, *the*

Fisherman's Joy, or spending time on her ship, so moving here was a vast change of lifestyle. It all felt so spacious. Perhaps in time she would get used to it, but at the moment it was all quite daunting.

Adam could see that Cat was nervous, but she was doing her best to hide it. Smiling, he walked over and joined her on the couch.

"I saw my sister yesterday, and she said you both enjoyed your recent trip to Cornwall." He commented, trying to make her feel at ease.

He noted the blush stealing over her cheeks before she answered, "Oh, yes, it was lovely. We both really enjoyed the fresh air."

For some reason, he had a feeling she was lying. For what reason he knew not, but he definitely felt it. He frowned, wondering what she was hiding.

"You stayed with your friend, didn't you?" He prompted.

"Yes, Abigail Meadows. She used to live in Portsmouth, like me, and when she invited me to stay, I couldn't resist. I asked Bess—I mean, Elizabeth—to come with me. We always have fun when we're together."

"I'm surprised Lord Maidstone didn't have something to say about that. Three weeks is rather a long time for his wife to be absent."

"I think he, um, had a journey planned at the same time." Cat said, vaguely.

"Cornwall's a damn fine place." Lord Fitzroy declared, taking a seat opposite them. "I used to know quite a few people down that way. I don't tend to travel much nowadays, though, not with this bad back of mine."

"Oh!" Cat said, her voice full of sympathy. "Isn't there anything the doctor can do?"

He shook his head. "Just rest, he says. But that doesn't seem to work either."

The maid arrived with the coffee and a tray of pastries. While she was pouring the drinks, Lord Fitzroy told them there was a ball being held that weekend at Lord Applegate's house, who was a neighbour of his.

"Perhaps you could accompany my granddaughter, Adam?" He turned his gaze on Cat. "Should you wish to go, my dear?"

"Oh. I think I might feel a little out of place. Perhaps when I have become more familiar with your friends, I...

He interrupted her. "But this is the best way to meet them, my dear. Adam will make sure you are well attended to, won't you, my boy?"

Adam cleared his throat, his green eyes twinkling with merriment. He would like nothing more than to spend some time with Cat, and this invitation was most fortunate.

"Miss Penley, it would be an honour to accompany you."

Cat's heart skipped a beat at Adam's request. The idea of attending a dance with him made her heart race, and she certainly didn't want to turn the opportunity down, but she also knew the challenges they would face due to societal expectations. Although she was the heiress to Woodleigh, she hadn't been brought up in high society and didn't really know if she would be accepted. What if she said something out of place or, worse yet, acted without decorum?

However, the allure of the dance and the prospect of spending an evening in Adam's company were difficult to resist.

A soft smile played on her lips as she met Adam's gaze. "Well, if you're certain, then I'd be delighted to attend the dance with you," she replied, her voice filled with sincerity. "I think I should feel a lot more at ease with you by my side."

She watched him smile, and he appeared to be genuinely pleased. She felt a shot of desire run through her as she realised that he appeared to return her feelings.

The maid handed her a cup of coffee, and as she went to accept it, her sleeve fell back slightly, revealing her wound. It was all but healed but still showed tight red skin around a small white scar.

"Oh, my dear, have you hurt yourself?" Lord Fitzroy exclaimed.

She immediately put her cup down and covered the scar with her hand. "Oh, it's nothing."

She realised Adam was frowning at her. "It looks quite sore. Have you had a doctor take a look at it?"

"Oh yes, of course. A doctor in Cornwall treated it for me. I assure you, it is fine."

"How on earth did you do such a thing, my dear?" Lord Fitzroy asked.

"Oh, I fell in the barn and caught my arm on something sharp on the floor." She held her arm out so they could see. "It is all but healed."

Adam peered at it and remarked in a low voice, "That looks like a nick you'd get from fencing. You don't fence, do you, Miss Penley?"

There was something in the intensity of his eyes that made Cat squirm. It was as though he could see straight through her lies. But she brazened it out. How could he possibly know?

"No, never."

He sat back in his seat. "Well, if you have any discomfort, I can send my own doctor over to attend you. You only have to ask."

"Thank you."

He stood up and smiled at her. "I'll take my leave and return on Saturday." Taking her hand, he kissed her knuckles before saying goodbye to her grandfather and leaving the room.

When he had left, Lord Fitzroy remarked, "He's a fine man. It's a shame he doesn't have a title, for he would make a good husband for you, but as it is, you will have to seek one in the higher echelons of society. It's why I wish for you to go to Lord Applegate's party. The cream of society will be there, and your wealth alone will have them vying for your attention. They will be like bees around honey; mark my words!" He laughed to himself, but Cat could find no humour in his words.

"I will never marry without love, Lord Fitzroy."

He smiled at her kindly and said, "There is no such thing, my dear. Not really. All you can hope for is admiration and appreciation."

Cat looked at him askance. "Didn't you love my grandmother?"

"No. She was tolerable, but no, I never loved her. I liked her, but that was all."

Cat stared at him, not knowing what to say. What a revelation. Perhaps this high society wasn't the place she should be. But one thing was certain: she would go to the party and judge for herself.

Chapter Two

The next day, Cat took the carriage to Lumley Hall. She wanted to see if Bess would accompany her to town so she could buy a new dress for the party or at least some new gloves. Anything to make her look as elegant as she could. Lord Fitzroy had told her to charge everything to his account.

Stepping out of the carriage, she was just in time to see Bess run past her at high speed. "Sorry, Cat, I won't be a minute!" She gasped, almost out of breath.

"But...!"

That was all she had time to say before Bill ran past. He raised a hand in greeting and, in three quick strides, captured his wife and pulled her back against his strong body.

Cat watched in fascination as Bess, her fiery co-captain, shrieked and tried to break free. But Bill was huge. No one, certainly not his small wife, would be able to break free from those massive arms.

He whispered something in her ear, and his large hand clamped on one of her buttocks. Cat winced. If she wasn't mistaken, Bess was going to be on the receiving end of those big hands very soon! She was often getting spanked because she rarely behaved.

Cat waited patiently, and soon, the pair of them turned around and walked over to greet her properly.

"Good afternoon, Cat," Bill said, smiling. "I trust you are well."

"Very well, thank you, Bill."

Bess was pouting, and her eyes were flashing fire. Bill looked down at her. "You only have yourself to blame, my sweet Bess. Now, I will leave you to talk with Cat."

He winked at Cat and sauntered away.

Cat looked at Bess and asked, "What have you done now?"

"Nothing much!" Bess declared, throwing her hands out in front of her, "He's just a great big lummox, that's all!"

Cat sniggered. "I thought married life would calm you down, but it hasn't, has it?"

Bess caught on to her humour and spluttered, "Not a chance, my friend, not a chance!" She grabbed Cat's hand and pulled her towards the front steps. "Come inside, and we can have a drink. I need a stiff rum."

Cat followed her up the steps and into the house. Lumley Hall was a lovely, big house that stood on its own grounds. Bess and Bill had decorated it lovingly, and it was every bit the home that Bess deserved.

Taking a seat in the parlour, Cat accepted the glass of rum that Bess handed her with relish.

She took a deep draught and smacked her lips. "That's a damn fine rum."

"Even more so, as it didn't cost a penny." Bess laughed. "We'll have to try and get some more next time—get a Frenchie. Their rum is the finest."

"Talking about that, Mr Clark said he's running low on supplies of liquor for the tavern. The customs men have been sniffing around again and have managed to confiscate some of his traders' wares. I told him I might be able to help."

Bess's eyes widened. "You didn't tell him you were a pirate, did you?"

Cat gasped, "Of course not! No, I simply told him that I knew a few people who might be able to obtain some liquor for him. Which, of course, is us! So, the next time we go, I'm hoping we'll come across a merchant ship with a hold full of alcohol."

"Ah, it'll be nice to help him out," Bess agreed, "and also outwit the bastard customs men."

"God, yes. When are you thinking of joining *the Blue Belle* again?"

"Well, it's the beginning of October, so how about the end of the month?"

"Sounds good to me."

"What will you tell Lord Fitzroy?"

"I think I'll tell him I'm going to Cornwall again. It worked last time." She frowned for a moment. "Although your brother didn't seem to believe me when I told him."

"You saw Adam?"

Cat nodded. "Yes, he was visiting Lord Fitzroy when I arrived yesterday. In fact, that's why I'm here." She leaned forward. "There's going to be a dance this weekend at Lord Applegate's house. He's a neighbour. I need to get something pretty at the boutique in town and wondered if you wanted to come with me."

"Oh, that's a great idea. I can keep out of Bill's way for a little longer. Delay the inevitable," she grinned.

"I don't know how you stand it." Cat said, shaking her head.

"Oh, it's not so bad, and the making up is fantastic." Her eyes sparkled with devilment, and Cat couldn't help but laugh.

"You're so naughty, Bess!"

"And you aren't?" Bess retorted, her eyes accusing.

"Well, maybe a little better behaved than you," she sniggered. "Did I tell you that Adam is accompanying me to the dance, and I can truthfully say I am very relieved."

"Relieved or excited?" Bess said, cocking her head and shooting her a knowing look. "I know you like him."

Cat looked coy for a moment and then said, "Well, I suppose you know me too well for me to deny it."

"I thought so. I've seen the way he looks at you as well. He most definitely likes you."

Cat's eyes grew soft, thinking of the handsome man, but then her face fell a little. "Lord Fitzroy told me that he thinks I need to marry a man with a title."

Bess's eyes grew hard. "I see, so he thinks that Adam isn't good enough!"

Cat nodded. "It shows you how little he knows me. But I've already told him I will only marry for love; I won't settle for anything less. I mean, imagine if you'd married Lord Fairchild!"

Bess grimaced. "Heaven forbid. That was a narrow escape, if you ask me. No, you should stick to your guns and only marry for love, Cat." She stood up and walked over to the table. Lifting up the rum bottle, she said, "Another?"

"Do you need to ask?" Cat grinned.

Lord Applegate's House

The elegant carriages lined up outside Lord Applegate's grand estate, their occupants stepping out in a flurry of silk and velvet. Cat, adorned in a beautiful gown of cream silk and lace, took a deep breath as she descended from the carriage, Adam at her side. The sounds of laughter and polite conversation filled the air, and she had the inclination to turn right around and go home.

She kept her hand on Adam's arm and whispered, "I'm so nervous!"

Adam looked down at her. "You have no need to be. You look quite stunning and will fit in perfectly."

She couldn't help the blush that stole over her cheeks. He was looking more handsome than ever, his dark hair swept back, and his attire was more than fitting for the occasion. She could feel his muscular form beneath the elegant fabric, and she felt a shiver of desire creep through her.

Whether he had a title or not, it didn't matter to her.

As they stepped into the lavish ballroom, she couldn't help but feel a sense of detachment from everyone around her. This was nothing like she was used to, and she wasn't sure she liked it. The polished manners and artificial smiles seemed foreign, a far cry from the camaraderie she had experienced with her crew on *the Blue Belle* or down at *the Fisherman's Joy* tavern.

The atmosphere in the large room felt a little suffocating, but she was determined to see how her new neighbours interacted with each other. Her grandfather wanted her to meet them, so she would do as he asked for now, but if they turned out to be arrogant bastards, then she would never make the effort again.

Cat's eyes scanned the room, taking note of the finely dressed men and elegant women. She noticed some of them set their eyes on her with unbridled curiosity.

Suddenly, a mature man approached them, his eyes warm. "You must be Miss Penley?"

Cat curtsied. "I am indeed, sir."

"Allow me to introduce myself. I am Lord Applegate." He studied her. "It's quite wonderful to finally meet you. Lord Fitzroy told me everything that happened, and I confess to being quite astonished!"

"I think we all were." She smiled at him. "May I introduce my friend, Adam Warren?"

Lord Applegate turned his gaze on Adam and smiled. "How do you do, sir? Welcome to Greatstone House."

He seemed like a very pleasant and genuine man.

Adam smiled in return. "Thank you."

A waiter came near, and Lord Applegate beckoned him over. "Try a glass of the punch. It's a family recipe and I think you'll enjoy it.'

Adam took two glasses and handed one to Cat. She immediately took a large mouthful, almost draining half the glass. "Oh, that's delicious."

She suddenly realised they were both looking at her, and her eyes widened. She was so used to drinking with Bess and the crew that she realised maybe she should have been a bit more refined. She placed a hand on her chest and said, "Oh, dear me! I was more thirsty than I thought. Do forgive me."

She saw Adam's lip twitch with amusement. Lord Applegate waved it away. "I'm not used to ladies drinking so quickly. It startled me for a moment. Perhaps I should get you another."

Cat felt her cheeks grow hot. "No, one is enough. Honestly."

"Well then, I will leave you to mingle."

When he had disappeared into the throng of people, Cat looked at Adam, her eyes wide. "Oh, Lord. I've only been here a few minutes, and he thinks I'm a drunkard!"

"I think you're just a little wilder than his usual acquaintances."

Cat laughed. "Maybe." She looked at him. "Do you think I'm wild?"

"Not wild, exactly, but you certainly know your own mind. There's nothing wrong with that." He took her drink off her and put it on the table nearby. "Now, Miss Penley, would you do me the honour of dancing with me?" He bowed theatrically.

"I should like that very much, Mr Warren." She answered, her eyes flashing with humour at his overly polite demeanour.

Adam swept Cat onto the dance floor. He could see that many guests were intrigued by her, obviously having already been informed as to who she was. Men and women alike kept glancing in their direction.

It made him even happier that he was by her side to support her. Even though she had a strong character, being in such an atmosphere must be daunting.

He looked down at her heart-shaped little face, and her striking blue eyes regarded him silently whilst they moved in perfect harmony with the music. His eyes lingered on her soft, plump lips, and he felt an overwhelming desire to kiss her.

When his gaze moved back to meet hers, he could see his own desire reflected in her eyes. He'd felt an attraction to her from the first day he'd met her, and now that he could see that it was returned, it heartened him.

He was thirty-two and had never felt the need to settle down before. In fact, he'd never met a woman that he could envisage living with until he'd met Cat. She was twenty-six, and she had the poise and intelligence that he'd been looking for. She was also quite feisty, another thing he admired about her. He wanted his wife to have a mind of her own, and Cat certainly had that.

The music ended, and he led Cat to the side. He was about to talk to her when a man approached. His eyes settled directly on Cat.

"May I introduce myself?" He bowed eloquently. "Lord Bowen."

Adam watched as Cat curtsied politely. "Miss Penley."

"May I have this dance?" the man asked enthusiastically.

Cat glanced at Adam, and he quirked an eyebrow. He could see the hesitation in her eyes, but Lord Bowen pressed the issue. "I do assure you, I'm quite accomplished!"

He held his arm out for her to take, and seeing as he was so eager, Cat agreed.

He watched the man whisk her away onto the dance floor and immediately felt a pang of jealousy. She was one of the finest-looking women in the room, and Adam realised, in that moment, that he had to marry her.

Chapter Three

Cat listened to Lord Bowen as he prattled on, wondering why on earth she accepted his invitation to dance, but he'd appeared so desperate that she didn't have the heart to turn him down. She resigned herself to her fate and kept a polite smile plastered on her face.

She had come here to meet people, so perhaps it wasn't a bad thing—the good with the bad—but Lord, he was boring.

As he led her around the dance floor, she could only think of one man, and that was Adam. She hadn't mistaken that look in his eyes earlier, and it had mirrored her own desire.

Her grandfather's words came back to her about not marrying him because he didn't have a title. Fie to that! If there was something Lord Fitzroy would have to understand, it was that Cat didn't capitulate easily when it came to affairs of the heart, and in this instance, not at all!

Her gaze inevitably found its way back to Adam. He stood at a distance, observing the proceedings with a mixture of amusement and patience. His presence gave her a sense of normality, and she couldn't wait to be alone with him, away from the curious glances and false smiles.

She almost wished she hadn't come, but then again, it had given her the opportunity to dance with Adam. Her cheeks grew rosy as she imagined what it would be like to kiss him.

"You dance awfully well, Miss Penley." Lord Bowen said, interrupting her thoughts. He was looking at her with obvious admiration, and Cat just stopped herself from grimacing. Oh, Lord, did he think her blushes were for him? That's all she needed. He was most probably only admiring her for her fortune anyway, or perhaps he did indeed find her captivating.

Either way, she wasn't interested.

Cat's frustration grew as the dance progressed, but she held onto the hope that she would soon find solace in Adam's company. He was the only one who saw her for who she truly was, beyond the trappings of her newfound wealth. Although even he didn't know everything, and she intended to keep it that way for now!

As the music ended, Cat quickly returned to Adam's side. "Can we go home?"

"You wish to leave already?" His deep voice showed concern.

She wrinkled her nose. "I just don't feel comfortable here."

He gave her a wry smile. "I know exactly what you mean." He held out his arm for her to take and began to lead her away, but their path was intercepted by an austere-looking gentleman.

"Miss Penley?"

Cat nodded.

"I have been looking forward to meeting you. My name is Lord Wentworth. I wonder, would you come and join me in the dining hall?" He looked at Adam. "And you too, sir."

"We were just about to leave," Adam said.

"Oh heavens, the night is young!" He declared and then, looking back at Cat, said, "You simply must come and talk to us. We've heard so much about you."

Cat hesitated. Her desire to spend some time alone with Adam was foremost in her mind, but Lord Wentworth seemed so sincere and insistent that she found herself agreeing.

"Well, I suppose it won't hurt to delay our departure a bit longer." She looked at Adam. "Is that alright with you?"

He smiled. "I have no objection."

So they followed Lord Wentworth out of the dance hall and along a grand hallway into a dining hall.

"Lord Applegate has a lovely house." Cat said, taking in the beauty of the high ceilings and elegant furniture.

"Oh, indeed, he does." Lord Wentworth agreed. "Ah, here we are." He led them over to a group of people and immediately introduced everybody, but for Cat, there was only one person that stood out, and that was Lord Wentworth's daughter, Lady Caroline. Her eyes sparkled with animosity as soon as she laid eyes on Cat, and the feeling was mutual.

Everyone else seemed very amiable, and Cat was bombarded with so many questions that it almost made her head spin. But smiling, she answered every one of them. A little while later, she looked around to see where Adam had disappeared to and found that he was standing next to Lady Caroline on the other side of the room.

Unbidden, a surge of jealousy ripped through her when she saw him throw his head back with laughter at something she said.

Making her excuses, she walked over to him, trying her best to remain composed and not give away her feelings. "Shall we leave now, Adam?"

"Of course, my dear," He turned to Lady Caroline. "Good evening, my lady."

Cat glanced at Lady Caroline and didn't miss the look she gave her. It was one of malice mixed with triumph.

Cat immediately bristled. Damn cheek! Did she think that Adam would be interested in a hoity madam like her? Cat shot her a look of barely concealed contempt and didn't bid her farewell at all. She didn't care if it would be considered rude. She just took Adam's arm and walked away.

A little while later, after bidding their host goodbye with a promise to return, Cat and Adam stepped out into the cool night air. The echoes of laughter and music slowly faded behind them, leaving a moment of tranquillity in their wake.

But Cat certainly wasn't tranquil. She was still smarting from the look that Lady Caroline had given her. She was after Adam; that was obvious. And he seemed just as taken with her. Why had he been laughing like that so easily? Was he taken with her?

Her eyes narrowed angrily, her jealousy threatening to break free.

"You seem rather quiet." Adam noted.

"Am I?" she huffed.

"Did something happen that I don't know about?" he asked, turning her around to face him.

"I don't know! Did it?" she snapped.

She watched his brow furrow, and a dark look came over his face. "Why have you suddenly got attitude?"

"I haven't!"

"Yes, you have."

She shrugged her arm from his and stormed off towards their waiting carriage. When he went to offer his hand to help her inside, she slapped it away. "I can do it."

She saw his jaw clench with anger out of the corner of her eye but ignored him and plonked herself down on the seat, keeping her face angled away from his.

He climbed in and sat opposite her. "Do you know you are this close to getting a spanking?" He said, eyeing her angrily.

She turned to look at him and gasped. "I would never let you spank me."

"You wouldn't get a choice." His eyes glittered with anger, and Cat could see the threat clearly in his eyes, so she wisely chose to remain quiet. Turning her head away, she kept her gaze averted as the carriage made for home, her bottom lip pouting with indignation.

Adam looked at Cat's stern countenance and wondered what could possibly have put her in such a foul mood. He could only surmise it was because he'd been speaking to Lady Caroline.

He smiled to himself. If that was the case, then it could only be because she was jealous. She looked even more beautiful in her jealous rage, her cheeks pink with indignation.

He reached out and took her hand. She turned to him in surprise.

"Cat," he said softly, looking into her eyes. "What would you say if I told you that I want to court you?"

"I thought you were too enamoured of Lady Caroline to think about me!" she huffed, still bristling.

So he had been correct. She was jealous.

Adam grinned and, raising her hand to his lips, grazed his mouth against her knuckles. "Just because I spoke to her doesn't mean that I'm in love with her. The only person I love is you."

Cat's heart skipped a beat at Adam's words. The sincerity in his voice and the intensity of his gaze stirred emotions within her that she didn't know were possible. Her jealous feelings quickly diminished, and a smile tugged at the corners of her lips as she met his gaze. "Adam, do you truly love me?"

"Yes, I do."

Their eyes locked, and she could see he truly meant what he said.

"I love you too, Adam. I have for a long time." She admitted.

Adam placed his hands around her waist and quickly drew her across the divide onto his lap. She looked startled for a moment, but when his lips touched hers, she was lost.

His kiss was firm and passionate. Time seemed to stand still as their connection deepened and the world around them melted away.

In that single, stolen moment, Cat felt a sense of belonging. His arms felt huge around her, and it made her feel small and safe. Now she knew how Bess felt. As much as they were both independent women, there was nothing like being in the arms of someone you loved.

As they pulled away, their breaths mingled in unison. "Cat, you have no idea how much this means to me," Adam stated, his voice firm yet quiet. "I've wanted to kiss you for so long."

"You have?" Cat's eyes sparkled with happiness.

He nodded. "In fact, I should do it again just to make up for lost time."

Before she could respond, his lips touched hers, and she was lost in a heady moment of desire.

Cat awoke the next morning to the sound of rain against the windowpane. She grimaced and pulled the covers over her head, trying to block out the sound. Eugh.

She stretched her limbs, feeling the warmth of the bed, and didn't at all feel like getting up. This was far too comfortable. If there was one thing she was definitely getting accustomed to about living at Woodleigh, it was the sheer comfort of everything. This bed alone was much bigger than her one at the tavern, and the mattress was so soft it felt like sleeping on feathers. Hence the reason she didn't want to move.

Thoughts of the previous night entered her mind, as did, above all, the knowledge that Adam loved her. She smiled, like the cat that got the cream, and decided that perhaps she should get up. She wanted to inform Lord Fitzroy of Adam's intentions towards her, and she was fully expecting resistance. She had told Adam to wait a few days before calling on her to give her time to clear the air, for she knew there would be a battle.

But she was used to battles, and a little conversation with Lord Fitzroy wasn't about to get her down!

Her maid, Sara, arrived, and soon Cat was dressed in a simple pale blue gown, her blonde hair neatly pinned and curled.

Making her way downstairs, she entered the dining room. Lord Fitzroy was already there; he sat at the head of the table and was engrossed in his morning newspaper. He looked up as Cat entered, his eyes lifting.

"Good morning, Catherine."

"Good morning, my lord," Cat greeted him. "Did you sleep well?"

Lord Fitzroy motioned for her to take a seat. "I did, my dear. I didn't hear you return last night, so I expect it was rather late. How did it go?"

As Cat settled herself at the table, she took a deep breath, gathering her thoughts. She knew that discussing Adam's request to court her would not be an easy conversation, so for now she would start off with small talk about the soirée.

She knew it would undoubtedly ruffle his feathers when she informed him of her intention to marry Adam, so she'd delay it a little longer.

"Lord Applegate was very pleasant and welcoming to both of us. I took an instant liking to him."

"Oh, indeed, he is a wonderful man. He lost his wife a few years ago; she was equally as nice. It was a sad time for everyone. But he pulled through with the help of his children." For a moment, his face grew grim, remembering the past, but then he pushed the sad thought aside and asked, "Were you introduced to anyone else?"

"Yes, Lord Bowen, Lord Wentworth, and Lady Caroline Wentworth."

"Ah, yes. Caroline is a bit spoiled but can be pleasant." He raised an eyebrow and looked away, muttering, "Nothing that a firm hand wouldn't have controlled when she was a child."

She was spoiled, alright, thought Cat. "How old is she?"

"Twenty-eight now, I believe. Rather old to be a spinster, but then no man so far has been good enough for the chit."

"Oh dear. I'm twenty-six; where does that leave me?" Cat giggled to herself whilst reaching for a piece of toast

"Ah, you have only recently arrived in society, my dear. You will soon be married; mark my words. You will have suitors galore coming to the house."

Cat decided to stop him right there. Now was the moment to reveal her romantic involvement with Adam.

With a steadying breath, Cat began, "Speaking on this subject, Lord Fitzroy, I must tell you that Adam has asked for permission to court me."

Lord Fitzroy's face shot to hers. "Adam?"

Cat nodded. Immediately, his face turned crimson, and he slammed his fist on the table, causing the silverware to rattle. "Absolutely not!" he exclaimed, his voice filled with anger and indignation. "Adam has no title, no noble lineage. He's not suitable for someone of your stature."

Cat's eyes flashed with defiance as she met Lord Fitzroy's gaze. She thought he might be angry, but this was off the scale. "Lord Fitzroy, titles and noble lineage mean nothing to me. Adam has proven himself to be a man of integrity and kindness who genuinely loves me. I absolutely refuse to let societal expectations dictate my happiness."

Lord Fitzroy's face grew redder, and he leaned forward, his voice sharp with authority. "You will listen to me, Catherine," he retorted. "I will not allow you to jeopardise your future and the future of Woodleigh Manor by associating yourself with someone so beneath you. It's my duty to protect your reputation and secure a suitable match." He narrowed his eyes. "And Adam Warren is most definitely not suitable!"

Cat's temper broke to the surface, and she leaned forward angrily. "With all due respect, Lord Fitzroy, my happiness should be of paramount importance. I refuse to sacrifice my heart's desires for the sake of a title. I love Adam, and he loves me. That is worth more to me than anything!"

The room fell into a tense silence as the clash of wills hung heavy in the air. Cat knew that her defiance would not come without consequences. Lord Fitzroy was a formidable force, and his disapproval could potentially sever their relationship. But she was willing to risk it all for the chance at true happiness.

Lord Fitzroy gave her a hard stare. "As much as I understand that you have strong feelings for Adam, and I can see why, for I like him too, you must understand the ramifications of your actions. Society will not look kindly upon such a match. You will be ostracised, and your reputation will be tarnished."

Cat's voice remained resolute, and her eyes filled with determination. "If being true to myself and following my heart means facing societal judgement, then so be it. I'm willing to face the consequences and fight for the love I believe in. What do I care about society?"

The rain continued to fall outside, mirroring the clash of emotions within the dining room. Cat and Lord Fitzroy sat staring at each other, neither willing to capitulate.

"I assure you," Lord Fitzroy said, "you will care about society when you have children. For they will be the ones to suffer in all this."

Cat had had enough. She rose from the table, her heart heavy but her fiery spirit unyielding. "I hope that you'll come to understand and accept my decision," she said, her voice filled with resolve. "And if you don't, then I shall simply return to my previous life as if nothing happened. I don't wish for it to be that way now that we've discovered one another, but I'm not willing to give up the man I love for other people's convenience."

Without waiting for him to reply, Cat left the dining room and headed back to her bedroom. Perhaps time alone would make him rethink his archaic views on married life. She highly doubted it, but that didn't mean that she was going to capitulate. Oh no. She loved Adam and intended for them to marry. In fact, the sooner the better!

Chapter Four

An hour later, and with the rain finally stopping, Cat decided she needed some fresh air. Her mind was in turmoil, and she really wanted to talk to Bess about it. She wasn't going to bother taking the carriage; she needed to feel the wind in her hair, so she made her way down to the stables.

A young lad, Oliver, greeted her. "Good morning, Miss Penley."

She'd already been introduced to him, but this was the first time she was going to take one of the horses out. "Morning, Oliver. Have you got a decent horse I can take out? I don't want a plodder!"

He laughed. "That's Samson off the list, then." She followed him as he walked along the line of stalls until he stopped in front of a fine chestnut mare. Cat's eyes lit up. "Oh, she's a beauty!"

"She is. She's fast n'all."

"What's her name?"

"Briony."

Cat raised her hand and stroked her nose. "Oh, you're beautiful." Briony snickered in response.

"I think she's taken to you already, Miss," Oliver remarked. "I'll have her ready in a moment."

Cat walked to the front of the stables and waited for him to get the tack ready for Briony. The rain had left the ground damp, but the temperature was still acceptable for early October. A ride out would do her good and hopefully improve her spirits.

Oliver led Briony out, and Cat quickly mounted the chestnut beauty. Thanking Oliver, she set off on a brisk ride towards Lumley Hall.

Half an hour later, with her hair hanging wildly about her shoulders, Cat arrived at Bess's house. She dismounted gracefully and handed Briony over to a stable lad before making her way up the wide steps to the house.

The butler greeted her with a warm smile. "Good day, Miss Penley. Do come inside."

"Is Elizabeth at home?" she asked.

"Yes, she's in the drawing room. Shall I show you in?"

"Yes, please."

Bess looked up as the door opened, and as soon as she saw Cat, her face lit up. "Cat! This is a surprise."

Hobbs left the room, and Bess immediately hugged her. "I was hoping you'd come soon. I am dying to know what happened last night at the soirée." She pulled away, and Cat saw that her face was adorned with a mischievous grin.

"What have you been up to?" Cat couldn't help but ask, for there was devilment in Bess's green eyes.

"Well, nothing much." Bess exclaimed, her eyes sparkling with a mix of amusement and defiance. "It seems I've once again managed to find myself in Bill's bad books."

Cat couldn't help but chuckle at Bess's spirit. "Oh, Bess, what did you do this time? Can't you stay out of trouble?" She teased, a light-hearted smile tugging at her lips. "Although, I'm sure you'll charm your way back into his good graces in no time."

Bess giggled. "I already have!" She walked over to a tall cabinet. "Now, does Madam require tea, or will a nice glass of rum suffice?"

"Rum!" Cat said, grinning.

After pouring two deep glasses of rum, Bess handed one to Cat and then sat down rather gingerly.

Cat quirked an eyebrow. "He spanked you again, didn't he?"

Bess nodded. "Stung like the devil. His hands are so large, Cat."

"Your brother threatened me with a spanking last night! What is it with these men?"

Bess's jaw dropped. "He did what?"

Cat nodded. "Have he and Bill been discussing how to punish women or something?"

"Well, it would seem that way." Bess said, frowning. She took a long drink of her rum and smacked her lips appreciatively. "Now then, what happened last night when you met your neighbours, and why on earth did my brother threaten you with a spanking?"

Cat took a deep breath and told her about the people she had met, including the spoiled Lady Caroline.

"So it was a rather interesting evening, but I could have done without her being present. You should have seen the way she looked at me when she thought I was a rival for your brother's affections. Damn cheek!" Cat pulled a face. "That's why Adam threatened to spank me—because I gave him attitude in the carriage. To be honest though, Bess, I was jealous!"

"I would have been too. I hate devious women like her. What happened after that?" Bess asked.

"Adam said he wishes to court me and that he loves me," she grinned. "And I love him just as much, Bess!"

"Upon my word! How exciting!" Bess exclaimed, her voice filled with genuine delight. "That's wonderful news."

Cat nodded, a soft smile playing on her lips. "Indeed it is, Bess. He understands me in ways I never thought possible. But, Lord Fitzroy... Well, suffice to say we had a bit of an altercation this morning! He vehemently opposes our courtship, Bess. He believes that Adam's lack of title makes him unsuitable for me. What nonsense!"

Bess frowned. "How did you respond?"

"I stood my ground. It got quite heated, but I didn't hold back. I told him that I'm quite willing to go back to my old way of life and that I won't be told what to do." She shook her head. "And that's exactly what I believe, Bess."

Bess reached out and clasped Cat's hand. "Cat, I totally agree. Why should you change your lifestyle to suit others and not yourself? I really believe that you and Adam are meant to be together. So don't let anyone or anything stop you!"

"Let's have another rum to celebrate." Cat suggested, enjoying the warm glow the liquor was giving her. Whilst Bess was pouring the drinks, she said, "Do you think I should tell Adam about *the Blue Belle*?"

Bess stopped what she was doing and looked at her askance. "Are you mad? Can you imagine? Not only will he have to deal with knowing his intended wife is a pirate, but then he'll have to find out his sister is as well." She laid a hand on her chest. "And not only that, but his brother-in-law is a pirate."

She brought the drinks over. "No, don't say a word. Not yet, anyway. I'll talk to Bill about it and see what he thinks."

Cat sighed. As much as she was determined to marry Adam, she knew that it was going to mean a lot of changes in her life.

Later that evening

The atmosphere during dinner that evening was tense and heavy with unspoken words. Cat and Lord Fitzroy sat across from each other, their gazes avoiding direct contact. The weight of the disagreement hung between them and neither was willing to stand down, until, with a heavy sigh, Lord Fitzroy threw his napkin down and stared at Cat with exasperation.

"Are you determined to go through with this marriage?"

Cat looked up, meeting his gaze. "Yes, I am."

His lips thinned, and then, with a heavy sigh, he sat back in his chair and thrummed his fingers on the table. "You remind me so much of your mother. She had the same stubborn nature. It was both infuriating and endearing."

"There is nothing wrong with knowing your own mind, my lord," she replied, her voice filled with determination. "I know my choices may seem unconventional and perhaps even reckless, but my feelings for Adam are too deep to just push aside."

Lord Fitzroy sighed, his stern features softening ever so slightly. "I cannot deny the sincerity of your feelings, Catherine," he admitted, his voice tinged with resignation. "Though it pains me to see you defy societal expectations, I cannot bear the thought of losing you completely. If Adam is truly the one who holds your heart, then who am I to stand in the way, I suppose?"

A sense of relief washed over Cat as she realised that Lord Fitzroy, despite his reservations, was willing to put their bond above his own desires. It was a small victory, but one that held great significance.

"Thank you, my lord."

"Isn't it about time you called me grandfather, my dear?"

Cat smiled. Yes, things were definitely changing for the better.

A few days later, Adam decided it was high time to visit Cat. She should have had time to talk to her grandfather about their intentions, and he wanted to know the outcome. He hoped he wouldn't have any objection, but somehow he feared he would.

Adam wasn't a poor man, not at all. He would inherit his father's house and be quite wealthy, but he didn't possess a title. He knew it didn't matter to Cat, but it could prove to be detrimental.

As soon as he arrived, Cat slipped her arm through his and led him into the private garden at the back of the house, where they sat down on a stone bench.

"You're looking very lovely today, Cat." He declared, looking at how fresh and pretty she appeared.

She blushed prettily. "Thank you, Adam." She then proceeded to tell him about her grandfather's reluctant acceptance.

When she had finished, Adam sat back, relieved. "It sounds like your achievement wasn't easy. I'll go and talk to him in a minute and prove to him that I have enough wealth to keep you in the manner to which you are accustomed."

Cat giggled. "Which isn't much when you consider I was living in the tavern for ten years!"

Adam smiled and took hold of her hand. "That's what makes you so special, Cat. You don't have the frivolous nature of most women that come from that society."

"Thank goodness." She looked at him for a moment, her blue eyes serious. "I have a question for you."

"Oh?"

"Well, it's more of a demand, really."

"Is it now?" He eyed her speculatively, wondering what she was going to say, and then she surprised him.

"I won't beat about the bush. Do you want to get married right away?" She stood up and paced in front of the bench. "I know that might seem a little forward of me, but I don't see the point in wasting any time. We have known each other for a while now, and we both love each other, and..."

Adam interrupted her by grabbing her wrist, pulling her straight down onto his lap, and kissing her firmly. She melted into his arms immediately, her lips parting to receive his tongue as it slid into her warm mouth.

A few moments later, they broke away, breathless. His eyes crinkled with mirth, and he said, "Does that answer your question?"

"Indeed it does, sir, indeed it does!" She laughed and snuggled into his chest.

"So do you want to leave the arrangements to me? We can get married at that quaint chapel in Somerstown." He suggested.

Cat drew back from him and said, "I think my grandfather would prefer his own chapel. If you don't have any objections?"

"No, not at all."

She suddenly looked a little coy. "There's another reason I want to marry soon. I'm going to Cornwall in a few weeks, and I'd like for us to marry before I go."

"Surely you can change your plans?" He asked. "I'm certain your friend, Abigail, won't mind. Besides, you can invite her to our wedding."

He noticed her cheeks turn pink, and she looked down at her hands. "Oh, she won't want to come. She's far too busy. That's why I usually visit her. Elizabeth is coming with me again."

Adam nodded. "I see."

He watched her eyes dart to his, and he knew she was hiding something, but he couldn't fathom what it was.

He decided that the next time he spoke to Lord Maidstone, he would find out if he knew anything. If his wife and Cat were up to something, he'd definitely know about it. For now, he decided to leave things alone. She could keep her secret for now.

"Three weeks apart will be a challenge, my love, but it will make our reunion even more heartwarming," he said, and taking her small chin in his hand, he raised her face and captured her lips once again, sealing their love.

Chapter Five

A week later

The lively sounds of laughter and clinking glasses filled the air of the bustling *Fisherman's Joy* as Cat sat at a dimly lit corner table, her eyes fixed on Mr Clark.

It felt comforting to be back in the familiar tavern again, a place she had lived in for so long. As much as she enjoyed the comfort of Woodleigh, the tavern would always have a special place in her heart.

Mr Clark was genuinely happy to see her, and lifting up the bottle of wine, he refilled her glass.

"Well, my dear, it heartens me to see you so happy. Adam is a fine man. I couldn't have chosen better myself."

"I'll raise my glass to that." She grinned, looking across at the man in question. He was talking to Albert, a regular at the tavern. He was very old but always managed to collar someone to have a conversation with, and in this instance, it was Adam. She caught his eye and smiled wickedly, knowing he was probably bored to tears. Albert did have a tendency to go on and on.

Cat looked around at the clientele. "It's very lively in here today."

"*The Lothian* is in port," Mr Clark replied. He gave a disapproving look. "As much as I like their patronage, they have a tendency to be very rowdy."

Cat nodded knowingly. "Ah, yes, *the Lothian*."

As if on cue, the jovial atmosphere suddenly took an abrupt turn when a raucous fight broke out between two drunken sailors nearby. Cat's instinct to intervene kicked in, and she jumped up automatically, her sense of justice compelling her to help diffuse the situation. However, before she could make a move, Adam appeared right next to her and firmly grasped her arm.

"Cat, come away," he commanded. "It's not safe."

Cat's eyes flashed with defiance as she shook off Adam's grip. "I won't stand idly by when there's trouble, Adam. I can take care of myself."

Ignoring his protests, Cat moved towards the commotion, her determined stride drawing the attention of the patrons. But before she could reach the fray, Adam swiftly scooped her up, lifting her off her feet and over his shoulder.

"Adam! Put me down this instant!" Cat hissed angrily, embarrassed at being treated like that in front of the customers. Thankfully, most of them were focused on the fight as even more sailors began to join the scrum.

Adam, unfazed by her protests, carried her through the tavern and up the stairs, finally depositing her unceremoniously onto the bed in her old bedroom.

He pointed his finger at her face. "You will obey me, whether you like it or not!"

Cat stared back at him and went to say something, but he waved his finger in her face. "No, Cat! Not another word."

She quickly snapped her mouth shut. He was deadly serious, and she knew she would be in serious trouble if she continued.

With a resolute expression, he left the room, closing the door firmly. She heard the lock click into place as he turned the key.

Cat's anger burned fiercely within her. She could handle that rowdy bunch easily; all she would have had to do was grab the big baton that Mr Clark kept behind the bar for just such an occasion, and she would soon have had them under control. She'd done it before often enough. Just one look at her wielding the great stick usually had them standing to attention—that, and the fact they'd be thrown out without any more drinks!

Angrily, she leapt from the bed and pounded on the door, demanding her freedom. She refused to be treated like a helpless damsel in distress. With a surge of determination, she decided to escape through the window.

She climbed onto the sill, her agile form squeezing through the narrow opening. With a careful grip, she clung to the drainpipe, her heart pounding with adrenaline as she descended towards the ground.

When her feet touched the solid path, she brushed her skirts down and turned around to run back into the tavern, but to her dismay, she found Adam standing there.

She gasped, her eyes widening.

His arms were crossed over his chest, and he had an angry expression etched on his face. "And where do you think you're going?" he demanded. "I thought I made it clear that you were to stay put."

For a moment, Cat felt intimidated, but then her frustration came to the fore, and she went to brush past him.

She didn't get far before he brought her to a standstill, his strong arm capturing hers. "You are too stubborn for your own good; do you know that?"

"I'm not a delicate little flower, Adam. I'm quite capable of helping Mr Clark to sort that bunch of ruffians out."

Adam shook his head. "I know you're strong and capable in some things, Cat, but these are rowdy sailors. They're not people you should be around. Besides which, ladies do not get involved in such manly brawls."

"I used to work here, or had you forgotten?" She snapped, glaring at him.

"Watch your attitude, Cat," he warned her sharply. "Mr Clark has already diffused the situation, so your help was not needed or desired."

His lips thinned with anger. "When I tell you to do something for your own safety, I expect to be obeyed!"

Cat took a deep breath, trying to control her temper. "I don't obey anyone!"

He placed his hand on her chin. "You will obey me, Cat." His eyes pierced hers. "Now, I'm going to take you back upstairs, and I'm going to give you a little lesson on how to behave. You can either go there of your own free will, or I'll put you straight over my shoulder again. The choice is yours."

Her stomach flipped nervously. He'd threatened her before with a spanking, but she never thought he would actually carry it out. "You can't do that."

"Do you doubt me?" He said, his eyes fierce with determination.

Cat's eyes widened, knowing he was deadly serious. "But Adam!"

"Well?"

Oh, Lord! What a choice he had given her. She certainly didn't want to enter the tavern over his shoulder; what a spectacle that would make, so it left her only one choice. She raised her eyes to the heavens, and then, huffing loudly, she stomped towards the tavern door.

Adam watched her go. Her back ramrod stiff, and her bottom lip pouting with self-pity. His eyes narrowed. She only had herself to blame. If there was one thing he wasn't going to stand for, it was Cat putting herself in danger.

Striding after her, he made his way up to her old bedroom. She was waiting for him outside the door, leaning against the wall with her arms folded and a sulky look on her face.

Suppressing a smile, he took the key from his pocket and unlocked the door, ushering her reluctant form inside.

Closing the door, he locked it for privacy and concealed the key in his pocket before turning to look at her. She was staring at him with a mixture of defiance and wariness.

He took one of the chairs and moved it near the bed before taking a seat. Her eyes darted from him to the door, and he could see she was trying to fathom a way to escape, but he had the key.

He held his hand towards her. "Come here."

Her eyes flashed to his and her jaw tightened. "You're being unreasonable. There's no need to go to such lengths to..."

"Spank you?" he said, interrupting her. "Oh, yes, there is. Come here now."

He watched her chest heave as she realised she wasn't going to escape a punishment, but still, she stood her ground, ever-defiant.

Cursing under his breath, he stood up and grabbed her arm. She struggled, pushing her hands against him to break free, but it made no difference.

"Let me go, Adam!" she shrieked.

Determined, he sat down again and drew her rigid form over his lap. He pulled up her skirts in a thrice and wrapping one solid arm around her waist, he parted her bloomers so her peachy little bottom was exposed. It was a beautiful sight, and he paused for a moment to admire the silky, round buttocks.

He laid his hand on her soft skin and stroked the surface. He heard her give a small sigh and realised she was enjoying his touch as much as he was. It still didn't stop his determination to punish her.

He brought his hand smacking straight down on her bottom and heard her give a sharp intake of breath before she yelped and kicked her legs. "Aow! That hurt!"

She threw her hand around to cover her bottom, and he pushed it away.

"Do that again, and I'll make this punishment even longer; it's your choice."

"I hate you!" she hissed, her voice tight with emotion.

"No, you don't. You're just mad that I'm holding you accountable for your behaviour. There's a big difference."

He brought his hand down again and again, reprimanding her in between each smack, listening to her yelps and whimpers whilst he dished out her punishment.

It was her own fault. All she had to do was obey him, so she only had herself to blame.

When her bottom was a deep shade of pink, he stopped and caressed her heated skin, listening to her panting as she tried to control the pain.

"You really do need to understand, Cat, that I won't tolerate disobedience. Do you understand?"

He felt her stiffen, ever-defiant, so he smacked her sharply. That made her respond!

"Yes, yes! I am just used to my independence, that's all."

He relaxed his grip around her waist and moved her so that she was sitting on his lap. She looked at him petulantly.

"Independence is all very well, my little wild Cat, but when that puts you in danger, then it is unforgivable. Do you understand?"

She looked down a little and mumbled, "I suppose so."

"There is no supposed 'so' about it. I won't tolerate it, and each time you think to defy me, I'll put you straight over my knee. No hesitation. So, be warned."

Cat looked into the stern eyes of the big, handsome man. Her bottom was on fire, but she found herself responding passionately to his dominant nature.

As much as the spanking had hurt, it felt rather lovely to have someone care about her so deeply. He was the perfect husband for her. Anyone with a weaker disposition than her own would soon bore her.

Either that or she'd run rings around them, and the marriage would soon fall apart.

Maybe it was better this way. Having a dominant partner who cared about her deeply enough to chastise her when needed was a good thing. Bess had such a man, and now she could clearly see the appeal.

Putting her arms around his neck, she leaned forward and kissed him. "I can't promise to behave, Adam, but I will try."

He put his muscular arms around her, enclosing her in a tight embrace before claiming her lips in a searing kiss. She opened her mouth, accepting his sliding tongue as it entwined with hers. Desire coursed through her veins, and she realised that marrying Adam was one of the best decisions she would ever make.

The day of Cat and Adam's wedding arrived swiftly. The small chapel on Lord Fitzroy's estate had been adorned with delicate flowers and soft candlelight, creating an intimate and almost dreamy atmosphere.

Cat stood at the altar next to Adam, her heart pounding nervously. She wore a gown of flowing silk, the delicate lace accentuating her elegance. She had never felt prettier or more feminine. She subdued a giggle as she pictured the crew of *the Blue Belle* if they could only see her.

On her other side stood Lord Fitzroy. He caught her gaze and smiled warmly. She was so happy he had finally come around to her way of thinking. It would make living at Woodleigh so much easier, with no hideous atmosphere to contend with. Adam was going to move in with her for now, and they would flit between his home in Somerstown, where his father lived, and Woodleigh.

She turned her attention to Adam, reaching for his hand. His hands felt so big compared to hers, and she immediately thought of Bess and Bill. Glancing over her shoulder, she scanned the chapel until she spotted them. It wasn't hard because of Bill's height. He was looking very smart as usual, and Bess was looking very pretty in a gown of cream silk edged with green lace and a green overlay. It accentuated her dark hair, and she looked quite gorgeous. She caught her eye and grinned before turning back around.

It was lovely to have her best friends present, and as the intimate ceremony began, Cat and Adam sealed their commitment to one another. The exchange of rings brought tears of joy to Cat's eyes, knowing that this symbol of their love would forever bind them together.

After the ceremony, the newlyweds and their guests moved to the grand reception held at Lord Fitzroy's estate. Woodleigh had been decorated most beautifully, which was to be expected because the staff had been rushed off their feet for the last few days, ensuring it was all up to Lord Fitzroy's expectations.

The air was soon filled with laughter and music as their wedding celebrations began. The festivities continued well into the evening, as friends and family toasted to the happiness and future of Cat and Adam.

As the night drew to a close, the newly married couple made their way to the West Wing of Woodleigh Manor. As soon as they stepped inside the bedroom, they fell on one another with a lust that had been restrained for far too long.

If Adam had thought his bride would be shy and demure, then he was wrong. Cat was eager to find out what making love was like and didn't want to waste a moment.

They fell onto the bed, and their eyes locking with desire, they quickly divested themselves of their clothes. A button popped off Adam's waistcoat in his haste, and Cat's dress tore a little, but neither cared.

Adam captured her lips and kissed her fiercely. She responded likewise, running her hands over his naked back and feeling every muscle beneath her exploring fingertips.

She arched her back as Adam's teeth grazed her neck and then moved lower down to her full breasts, laving his tongue over the taut peaks. The feeling was exquisite. When his hot tongue flicked over her sensitive folds, she gasped with delight.

"Oh, Adam! It is too good!"

His large hands cupped her bottom, and he began a sensual assault on her small nub of desire, running his tongue over and over her slick folds. Keeping a steady pace that soon had her mind soaring up into the clouds as her small cries of delight filled the air.

Adam could hardly believe how sensual his wild Cat was. He had thought her kisses responsive during the lead-up to their wedding, but never would he have dreamed that she would respond to his lovemaking so passionately.

Her eyes were soft and sensual as she came down from her orgasm, and Adam quickly rose up and captured her lips.

"You are beautiful, Cat." He murmured, running his hands down her silky, smooth skin. Cupping one buttock, he positioned himself at her entrance and slowly began to push inside her slick, inviting warmth.

He tried to be as sensitive as he could, knowing that her first time could be painful, but she only tensed briefly, and then he was fully inside. Slowly, he began to move his hips and marvelled at her eager response.

She gripped his shoulders with her small hands, encouraging him and raising her legs; she wrapped them around his waist, urging him onwards.

"Please, Adam!"

She knew what she wanted and didn't hold back, her small cries of pleasure filling the air. Moving faster, he pumped his hips against hers, piercing her with his thick weapon again and again until, with a small cry, she orgasmed once more.

Adam could wait no longer and finally allowed himself the pleasure of release. Collapsing over her, he sighed loudly, utterly replete.

They lay quietly, letting their breathing calm before he rolled onto his side, taking her with him, his big arms holding her tight.

"Oh, my." Cat breathed softly. "I never thought lovemaking could be so good."

"We shall have to do it often." He grinned and then kissed her slowly, thinking as he did that she had the most kissable mouth he had ever known.

He broke away and looked into her beautiful blue eyes. She was staring back at him with a sultry smile.

"I like kissing you," she admitted.

"Then I had better do that often, too." He smiled, and with a growl, he drew her beneath him and captured her lips against his own, demanding a response, which she readily gave.

Chapter Six

A few days later, Cat took a ride out to visit Bess. Adam had left early in the morning for London, but only after ensuring his new bride was fully satiated. She sighed as she remembered how he had quickly brought her such pleasure.

He wouldn't be back until the evening, so she'd decided to sort out any final arrangements with Bess for their next voyage. They were due to sail out in a few days.

She pouted her bottom lip, wondering how she was going to endure being away from her husband for a few weeks, but her love of adventure out on the ocean was a hard desire to deny herself.

Besides, absence makes the heart grow stronger, although it wouldn't make it any easier.

Urging Briony into a canter, she headed out to the open fields. It was the beginning of November, and already some of the trees had lost their leaves, but even so, the sun cast its warm glow, making everything look quite beautiful.

The only thing that really marred her day was the fact that Lord Fitzroy had informed her that Lord Wentworth and his horrendous daughter, Lady Caroline, would be coming for dinner that night.

Her mouth curled as she pictured Lady Caroline's face. Lord. How was she going to endure listening to her prattle on, and if she so much as glanced at Adam with affection, she would make her regret it.

She tried to quell the anger that surged in her breast. Adam was already her husband; she had nothing to worry about in that regard, but it still didn't stop her from feeling jealous.

Shaking her head, she pushed the thoughts of the odious woman aside and directed Briony towards Lumley Hall.

That evening

Cat paced her bedroom in the west wing and then walked over to the window again, looking out onto the gravel driveway below. Adam still hadn't returned home, and Lord Wentworth was due any moment.

A knock came on the door, and she walked over to open it. It was Sara, her maid.

"I came to see if you needed any help, Madam."

"Oh, yes, please. Can you pin my hair for me? You always make it look so pretty."

Cat sat down on the seat in front of the dressing table, and Sara immediately started brushing out her hair.

"Have you met Lady Caroline before, Sara?" Cat asked her.

She nodded and almost winced. "Yes. She came to visit with Lord Fitzroy a few months ago. She is quite demanding."

"From the little I've seen of her, that doesn't surprise me." Cat declared. "I really wish I didn't have to attend tonight."

"Oh, I'm sure it will be fine. If things get too bad, you could always feign illness." Sara giggled, catching her eyes in the mirror.

Cat laughed back. "You're so right!"

Sara finished her hair and stood back to admire it. "Oh, you do look lovely, Madam." A noise made her look towards the window, and she rushed over. "The guests have arrived."

"And still no sign of my husband. Oh, well, wish me luck."

The elegant dining room was adorned with flickering candlelight as Cat took her place beside her grandfather.

"Adam still not home?" he asked, frowning.

"No, grandfather. It must be something serious to take his attention away from us."

"Hmmm," he grumbled, showing his disapproval.

Perkins, the butler, opened the door and presented Lord Wentworth and his daughter. Cat greeted them with a polite smile, and Lord Fitzroy exchanged pleasantries, offering them a drink before dinner.

Lady Caroline looked around and, directing her words at Cat, said, "I thought your husband was going to be here tonight."

"He's been delayed in London."

"Oh?" She quirked an eyebrow. "You'd have thought he'd want to be by his wife's side, but then perhaps his work is more important." Her words dripped with subtle venom, and Cat immediately bristled.

"His work is very important, and I'm fully understanding of that."

"Well, that's just as well, because it seems you don't have much say in the matter."

Before Cat could respond, she raised her glass and imperiously asked the butler for a refill.

Cat did her best to suppress her anger, knowing that it would do her no good to show the spoiled woman that she had got to her. No, she would remain calm for now.

Dinner was called, and they made their way to the table.

Cat was seated opposite Lady Caroline and maintained her composure throughout the many courses, responding with grace and poise to any questions that Lord Wentworth put to her. She even managed to bite her tongue at Lady Caroline's snide remarks. It was difficult, but she endured it, for she had already plotted a way of taking revenge.

As the dessert course was cleared away, Lord Fitzroy suggested a walk around the gardens. He'd had lanterns put strategically around so they could all enjoy an evening stroll.

"I should like that very much." Lord Wentworth said, standing up.

Cat excused herself; this was the opportunity she had been waiting for. "I'll join you in a moment. I'm just going to get a shawl; the air is a bit fresh this time of year."

With a calculated look in her eye, she made her way upstairs and into her bedroom, where she soon found what she was looking for: her slingshot. Picking up a few small wooden balls, she walked over to the window and very quietly opened it, waiting for the moment when Lady Caroline would walk past.

Adam entered through the large wrought iron gates at Woodleigh, just as night began to fall. He was a bit saddle-sore, but nothing a good hot bath wouldn't cure.

He'd hoped to be home earlier, but one of his clients, Lord Parkington, had detained him longer than expected. Being a lawyer, it sometimes came with the job. But he couldn't say he was that upset about missing dinner. Although he liked Lord Wentworth, the same couldn't be said for his daughter.

Thinking of her made him remember Cat's dislike of her through jealousy. Perhaps now that she was married, she would see Caroline for the spoiled girl that she was and not as a rival for his attention.

As he made his way up the long driveway, he could see Lord Fitzroy and Lord Wentworth walking towards the gardens, Lady Caroline trailing behind. He frowned, wondering where Cat was, and then all of a sudden, a piercing scream filled the air.

Lady Caroline was clutching her bottom, with her mouth gaping wide and a look of complete shock and pain on her face.

Adam looked up just in time to see his bedroom window close. What on earth had just happened?

He urged his horse into a canter and quickly dismounted, throwing the reins to Oliver, the stable boy.

"Whatever is the matter, Lady Caroline?"

She gulped. "Something just hit me!"

"What was it, dearest?" Lord Wentworth asked, rushing over to her.

"I don't know, but my derriere stings most painfully, Papa. I think I'll go back inside."

"Let me assist you." Adam said, holding his arm out. It was the least he could do.

She blushed a little and linked her arm through his. She walked rather stiffly back towards the house, and it was then that Cat appeared.

She locked eyes with Adam's, and there was the briefest flicker of alarm, but she quickly hid it. "Oh, Adam, you've returned!"

"Yes," he said, eyeing her speculatively. "It would seem Lady Caroline has been stung by something."

Lady Caroline, her face flushed with embarrassment and fury, attempted to regain her composure in front of Cat. "It felt more like a stone hitting me than a sting. It's most painful!"

"Oh, dear. Come inside." Cat said, wearing an innocent expression.

Adam wasn't fooled, though. He'd seen that look in her eyes, and he was never mistaken. Somehow she'd been involved, and by hook or by crook, he'd find out. He watched her lead Lady Caroline back into the house and went to follow them, but he trod on something small.

Frowning, he leaned down and picked it up. It was a small wooden ball. His eyes narrowed, and without raising suspicion, he put it inside his jacket pocket. He had a feeling it would come in useful later on.

Cat knew she was in trouble just by the look in Adam's eyes. Now all she had to do was profess her innocence. Bess managed to do it, so why shouldn't she?

A little while later, she stood on the stone steps, waving goodbye to their guests as the carriage started rolling away from the house, trying her best to look unfazed.

She felt Adam slip his arm around her waist, and quietly, so that Lord Fitzroy couldn't hear, he said, "I think you and I need to have a discussion, my dear. I'll lead the way."

Oh, Lord!

They both bid goodnight to her grandfather and made their way to their quarters in the west wing. Cat tried to calm her nerves, but it was hard. She had fought battles at sea and made captains blanche, but that was nothing compared to her formidable husband.

Walking into their quarters, Adam placed his hand in the middle of her back and manoeuvred her into the bedroom and towards the window. Standing next to her, he looked down at the drive below, nodded to himself, and then turned to stare at her.

"So, are you going to come clean and tell me what happened, or are you going to beat around the bush and deny any involvement?"

Cat swallowed hard. "I don't know what you're implying!"

"Of course you don't." Taking her hand, he reached inside his jacket and pulled out one of her slingshot balls, placing it in the palm of her hand. "Now tell me, you don't know what I'm talking about."

As much as she tried to brazen it out, her face flushed guiltily, but she still tried. "I have no idea what this is. A ball? What's it from?"

"I would suggest it's from a slingshot."

"What would I be doing with such a thing?" She said, her eyes flashing with indignation. "Ladies don't carry that sort of implement."

"Then why did I see our bedroom window close just after Lady Caroline got hit?" He walked over and placed his hand on her chin, angling her face to his. "This will go a whole lot easier if you tell the truth, because, believe me, I am going to punish you either way."

Cat's eyes widened. "Punish me?"

He nodded and removed his jacket. Then, silently, with his eyes fixed on hers, he began to roll his sleeves up. For a moment, Cat was transfixed. She loved his muscular arms and briefly forgot why she was even there as a wave of desire washed over her.

But then her eyes shot to his again, and she saw the determination within. Quickly, she made a dive for the door, but he was on her in seconds.

"And where do you think you're going, my little wild Cat?"

He lifted her up as though she weighed no more than a feather, and she soon found herself face down over his lap as he sat on one of the bedroom chairs.

She struggled, but it made no difference. He was far stronger than her, and soon her skirts were thrown over her back, and her bloomers parted.

"Oh Adam! This isn't fair!"

"You should have thought about that before launching a missile at Lady Caroline's backside!"

"I didn't!" She spat through gritted teeth.

"You did. You must know by now that I can spot a lie a mile off, and you, my dear, are most definitely lying!"

His hand settled on her bottom, squeezing one cheek as he admired the silky, smooth skin. Cat closed her eyes, loving his touch, but then she opened them wide and gave a loud gasp when he gave her a sharp spank.

"Ouch!" She yelped.

She tried to scramble off his lap, but his other hand hugged her tight against his hips. She wasn't going anywhere!

He set up a steady pace, spanking each cheek in turn, and no amount of protests or yelps from her made even the slightest difference.

Lord, it hurt! Why had he returned at the precise moment she'd pulled her stunt on Lady Caroline? It just wasn't fair!

She winced as he caught both buttocks at the same time in a swinging smack. "Aooow!"

"You only have yourself to blame, my little wild Cat. I don't know what possessed you to act in such a manner, but let me tell you now, it won't happen again."

Another few smacks from his large hand, and he finally stopped.

Cat lay panting over his lap, trying to control the pain. Her backside was on fire! She felt him relax his hold around her waist, and then he lifted her up to sit on his lap. His eyes bore into hers, stern and disapproving. "Go and get me that slingshot."

She thought about disobeying him, but when his brow furrowed, she knew what would happen if she did. So she stood up and practically flounced to her wardrobe and, groping around, found the slingshot where she had hurriedly hidden it earlier.

When she turned around, he was holding his hand out, and reluctantly, she handed it to him. He turned it over in his hands, inspecting it. "Where on earth did you get this, Cat?"

"From a friend," she pouted. That friend being Bess. But she certainly wasn't going to reveal that to her husband!

He shook his head and put it on the floor before grabbing Cat's hand and pulling her back down over his lap. She gasped as she found herself staring down at the floor once again. "But I've been punished already!"

"I'll decide when your punishment is finished, not you."

He drew up her skirts and untied her bloomers, lowering them to her ankles. She screwed her face up, waiting for his hand to make contact, but when it did, it was to knead her heated flesh, not spank it.

The feeling was exquisite. The fiery sting had abated a little, and the combination of his gentle strokes on her tender buttocks was setting her body on fire. She moaned softly, unable to quell her obvious desire, and her thighs parted invitingly, seeking his attention.

Adam didn't disappoint. She felt one thick finger slip sensuously between her slick folds, gently stroking her feminine core. His other hand squeezed her buttock, keeping her in place as he began a steady rhythm to give her the utmost pleasure.

The sizzling heat in her bottom, combined with Adam's firm hand, soon had her body soaring in ecstasy, her mind reeling at the thin line between pain and pleasure. Her small cry of pleasure filled the air, but before she had time to come down from the heady excitement, Adam picked her up and moved her to the bed, putting her face down, her bottom exposed on the edge, her feet on the floor.

She clutched the covers, her whole body alive with need. The need to feel him inside her. Dominating her as only he knew how.

Seconds later, she felt his thick shaft at her entrance, and then, his large hands gripping her hips, he pushed inside her. She gasped. He felt so big and full that she felt her orgasm begin to build immediately, and as he withdrew and pushed in again, her whole body ignited in fire. A fire that only he could extinguish.

She buried her face in the coverlet as he began a steady rhythm, seeking to bring them both pleasure, his thick length ramming into her again and again.

She cried out as another orgasm ripped through her, and soon after, she felt him tense, and with one final thrust, he groaned as he gave in to his own release.

Collapsing over her back but mindful of his weight, he kissed her neck. "You are too damn beautiful to resist, Cat."

She stretched beneath him, pushing her bottom back against him. The tender buttocks zinged to life, but the feeling wasn't unpleasant. "Why, husband, whoever said you had to resist me?"

She felt his cock stir again within her sheath, and with a low growl, he began to move his hips, drawing even more pleasure from his winsome wife.

Chapter Seven

A few days later

Cat and Bess had arranged to meet on *the Blue Belle*, anchored in a small cove near Portsmouth. It had only been a few days since they last saw each other, and Cat laughed to herself, knowing that Bess would want to know how her evening with Lady Caroline had gone. And on that front, she had a lot to tell her.

As Cat stepped onto the deck, she was greeted by the familiar faces of her loyal crew. They were standing to attention, their expressions guarded, and if she wasn't mistaken, they were looking rather mischievous.

Suddenly, McGregor boomed out, "Now, lads!"

Before she could fathom what was happening, they each lifted up their arms and threw a handful of rice all over her. She winced and put her hands over her face for protection, laughing at their boisterous behaviour.

"Good Lord, you rowdy lot!" She half complained, laughing at their antics.

The crew gathered around her, eager to bestow their well wishes upon their captain.

"Congratulations on your marriage, Captain!" McGregor said, his eyes twinkling with mirth. "I hope your new husband's up to the job."

"What do you mean, McGregor?" Cat queried.

"Well, it ain't every day a man finds himself married to a pirate captain!"

Before Cat had a chance to reply, Jasper, the ship's first mate, exclaimed, "We're heartened to hear about your marriage, Captain, and we hope you'll be very happy." His voice was filled with genuine happiness.

Cat smiled, touched by their warm wishes. "Thank you, everyone. I must admit, the last few weeks have been very exciting, but now I'm ready to set sail again and plunder a few of those tasty merchant ships! Is Bess here yet?"

Griffin shook his head. "She sent a message saying she'd be here at nightfall. So I'll take the tender to meet her on the beach."

McGregor's brows furrowed in confusion. "Captain, forgive me for prying, but shouldn't your husband be here with you? It's unusual for a newly married woman to be sailing the high seas without her spouse."

Cat's smile faltered for a moment, her mind racing to find the right words. "You see, McGregor," she began cautiously, "Adam is not aware of my... endeavours as a pirate captain. I haven't told him yet, so this part of my life is a secret."

The crew's surprise was palpable, their eyes widening in disbelief. McGregor, in particular, couldn't hide his astonishment. "You mean to say that your husband has no idea about your true identity?"

Cat nodded, her expression tinged with guilt. "I know it may seem deceitful, but I wanted to protect him from the dangers that come with my life as a pirate captain. I thought that by keeping this secret, I could give him less opportunity to worry."

McGregor looked at her knowingly. "Or maybe you didn't tell him because he might put a stop to your life on the high seas?"

Cat shot him a look of rebuke. "You don't know everything, McGregor!"

"Aye, I do!"

She thought about arguing back but knew it was useless. He was very astute and already knew the truth. She loved this way of life, and even though she loved Adam, she had a feeling he would never be able to accept her love of adventure and excitement that piracy gave her. It was a very dangerous game, but she loved it.

McGregor placed a hand on her shoulder. "Captain, although I trust your judgement at sea, keeping such a significant secret from your husband is a tad on the reckless side. But then it ain't none of my business."

Cat folded her arms across her chest and said mulishly. "No, it isn't!"

He ignored her and continued, "I mean, honesty is the foundation of any successful marriage, and you're doing the exact opposite!" He looked at her shrewdly.

Cat sighed, her shoulders slumping with the weight of his words. "Alright, alright. I give in. I know you're right, but I just don't know how to tell him. Not yet. I mean, obviously, I will at some point. Just not yet!" She glanced at his face and snapped, "Don't judge me, McGregor!"

He raised his eyebrows. "I'm just trying to warn you, Captain. Keeping secrets from your husband doesn't bode well for your future. That's all I'm saying!"

He walked away, mumbling to himself, and Cat's bottom lip pouted. The rest of the crew dispersed, going about their duties and preparing the ship to set sail as soon as Captain Bess came aboard.

Cat walked to the railing and looked out to the horizon, feeling more than a little confused. She had been so resolute in her conviction not to tell Adam about her secret life, but now McGregor was making her feel guilty.

She would talk to Bess when she arrived. She didn't have such a problem with her husband, seeing as Bill was a pirate himself. Cat thrummed her fingers on the railing, deep in thought, and then, huffing under her breath, she crossed the deck and entered her cabin. The only thing to tame a restless mind, in her humble opinion, was a tasty shot of rum!

Nightfall, high tide

As *the Blue Belle* sailed through the channel, Cat and Bess found a moment of respite to discuss Cat's dilemma. The wind whipped through their hair as they stood at the helm, their voices carried away by the vastness of the ocean.

"Bess," Cat began, her voice tinged with worry. "Do you still think I'm doing the right thing by not telling Adam about our life at sea?"

Bess nodded. "Absolutely!"

"But you don't have any secrets from Bill."

"Only because we're both in the same trade, or should I say the same boat?" Bess laughed out loud. "No, seriously, if you tell him what we do, it could ruin your marriage. Not only that, but he would find out about me and then Bill. Oh, dear me, no. Keep quiet for now and only tell him if you have to."

Cat's gaze turned towards the horizon, feeling a little bit better. "You're right, Bess. It'll only lead to trouble."

Bess nudged her. "Talking of trouble, how has your first week as a married woman been?"

Cat blushed. "Adam has been perfect. You have a wonderful brother."

"I wouldn't go that far." Bess grinned.

"Truly, everything has been perfect. Apart from the fact he spanked me!"

Bess's eyes widened. "He didn't?" She clapped a hand to her mouth, suppressing her laughter. "What on earth did you do to warrant a punishment? It must have been something bad."

Cat saw the funny side and explained the circumstances. Bess patted her on the shoulder. "Welcome to married life with a dominant husband."

"I did enjoy the making up, though." Cat giggled.

"You see, there's always a plus side."

"I suppose that's why I'm feeling guilty about keeping my life as a pirate secret, but it won't be forever. I guess there will come a time when we both decide to give this life up. But for now, I'm happy with things just the way they are."

"You and I both." Bess stated.

Cat glanced at her. "How are things between you and Bill?"

"Very good. I actually managed to avoid a spanking last week."

"You behaved for a change?" Cat said, her eyebrows raised, "Then I heartily congratulate you. That was some achievement."

Bess shook her head. "No, I didn't say that I behaved, only that I managed to avoid a spanking. There's a difference!" She sniggered.

"Oh, lord. I should've known."

"You see, whilst he was out, I borrowed his pistol. I was intrigued because it's heavier than ours, and I wanted to try it out. So, I took it around the back of the big barn and aimed for a bottle on top of that big sherry barrel he acquired..."

"I think I know where this is going!" Cat said, wide-eyed.

Bess looked a bit sheepish and continued, "Well, I took aim, and somehow I was off-cock; I think it was the weight of the bloody thing, and I blew a massive hole in the barrel."

Cat clapped a hand to her mouth. "Oh my God!"

"Exactly! The sherry is no more!" Bess collapsed against Cat, laughing like a drain.

"How the hell did you manage to convince Bill that you weren't involved?"

"I quickly put the gun back, saddled my horse, and went into town. I didn't return until late in the evening, as I knew he'd be home by then. So it looked like I'd been out all day. I just declared that it was a terrible thing to have happened and expressed lots of concern, and it worked out fine."

"Oh dear, poor Bill. I bet he was as mad as hell."

Bess grimaced. "That was an understatement. I think my backside would have suffered highly for that little mistake."

"I wouldn't call it little, Bess." Cat grinned. "Oh dear, I don't think you'll ever behave. Come on, let's go inside. McGregor's on watch, and I fancy a tipple before bed."

"A splendid idea."

Days passed, and *the Blue Belle* continued its journey across the open waters. The crew prepared for their next raid, eager for the spoils that awaited them.

As the sun dipped below the horizon, signalling the approach of twilight, Bess spotted a merchant ship on the horizon. Lowering her spyglass, she called across to Cat, her voice full of excitement. "This one looks ripe for the picking, Cat!"

Cat quickly joined her and, taking out her spyglass, scanned the horizon until her eyes fell on the fine-looking merchant ship. "Oh, yes," she agreed. "You'll do nicely!"

Anticipation filled the air as they plotted their attack, shouting out commands, and McGregor's loud voice called for all hands to be ready.

Cat grinned to herself. There was nothing quite like the prospect of plundering a merchant ship. Stealing from the rich and keeping the customs men from taking their greedy share by way of taxes.

She thought about Mr Clark and her promise to supply him with alcohol. Hopefully, this ship would have plenty on board.

"Raise the flag!" She shouted. "Show them our colours!"

As *the Blue Belle* closed in on the merchant ship, a section of the crew noticed something amiss and expressed their concerns to McGregor.

He appeared by Cat's side and said, "Captain, take a look at the crew. They don't look like ordinary sailors to us."

While she raised her spyglass again, he continued, "They look well-trained and well-armed, possibly ex-military."

Cat peered at the men. It seemed McGregor was right. They looked extremely smart and focused. She moved her spyglass along the hull until she came to the name, and she whispered to herself, "*The Malvernian.* We haven't encountered her before."

Bess joined them and said worriedly, "Do you think we should run?"

Just as she finished speaking, *the Malvernian* unleashed a barrage of cannon fire straight at them.

Caught off guard, *the Blue Belle* found itself in a perilous situation. The merchant ship's cannons ripped through the hull, disabling their ability to fight back effectively. Chaos ensued as the crew desperately tried to defend their ship, but the odds were stacked against them.

With several wounded and the hull breached, they were close to finding themselves at the mercy of *the Malvernian,* not the other way around, as intended.

Several burly merchant crewmen swung onto *the Blue Belle* and began a vicious attack. Bess fought alongside McGregor as one burly sailor lunged at them. He was not only massive, but also his sword skills were second to none.

Amidst the chaos, Cat found herself facing a formidable opponent alone. He was a skilled adversary, and even with her honed skills, he soon managed to capture her, his grip firm and unyielding. Cat fought valiantly, but her efforts were in vain as she was forcibly taken away from the safety of her ship as he swung across the divide.

She struggled and kicked, but the man was huge; she had no choice but to do as he said. Landing on the deck, she soon found her hands tied behind her back and a gag put across her mouth.

Her eyes sparked fire, but her perpetrator just laughed. She looked across to *the Blue Belle* and saw Bess standing at the railing, her eyes wide with shock.

McGregor, enraged, pushed his opponent straight over the railing and rushed over to join Bess, his eyes quickly locking with Cat's.

"What the devil!" He growled.

The merchant captain blew his whistle, and his crew quickly swung back over to his ship. Cat was shoved forward, and the captain stared at her with malice.

"My, it would seem you're all out of luck!"

Cat glared at him and tried to swear, but the gag just made her words come out as a pathetic growl. The captain laughed and, pushing her forward to the railing, called across to Bess.

"If you wish your captain to remain unharmed, then I suggest you leave now while you have the chance. My cannons are ready to finish the rest of the job and put your sorry ship at the bottom of the ocean."

Cat felt true terror. Not only for the crew of *the Blue Belle* but also for the thought of being left behind. But that decision wasn't hers to make.

She glanced down the hull of the ship and could clearly see *the Blue Belle* was taking on water. They had to leave. They had no choice. Not unless they all wanted to die.

Cat's terrified eyes locked with Bess. She knew Bess had to make that difficult decision to retreat. *The Blue Belle*, battered and broken, could withstand no more from the superior cannons on the merchant ship. The lives of the whole crew were at stake.

Cat watched as her beautiful ship limped away, fighting back tears and wondering how the hell she was going to escape.

Chapter Eight

Adam sat at his desk in London and thrummed his fingers on the polished wooden surface. He couldn't concentrate on his work today, not one bit, and it was all down to his wife.

It had all started that morning when he'd searched the bedroom wardrobe for his brass watch chain. He'd dropped it in there the night before and had been too tired to locate it, so he'd left it until this morning.

Cursing to himself, he'd finally found it lodged between two boxes, and with a quick tug, he'd managed to pull it out, but in the process, he knocked one of the boxes over. As it tumbled out onto the floor, the lid popped off, and to his surprise, a pistol had fallen out.

He'd stared at it in shock for a moment before reaching down and picking it up. It was a fine-looking weapon, and as much as he admired it, he wondered what the hell it was doing amongst his wife's possessions!

Why did she feel the need to have a weapon? Could she fire it? He looked down at the box and wondered what else was hidden inside. It didn't take him long to find two pairs of men's breeches.

Now he was truly confused. Was she having an affair? Why would she have men's breeches in her wardrobe? What was she hiding?

He had thought to confront her about it when she returned home, but that wasn't for another couple of weeks, and his suspicious mind couldn't wait that long. He needed someone to talk to about it, someone he could trust, and that was Lord Maidstone.

Rising from his desk, he grabbed his hat and coat from the stand and headed for the door.

Bill was surprised to see him when he was shown into his study later that afternoon.

"Adam, what brings you here?" Bill asked, stepping aside to allow him entry.

"I need to talk to you about Cat," Adam replied, his tone concerned. "Something unexpected has come to my attention, and I'm not sure how to approach it."

Curiosity gleamed in Bill's eyes as he offered Adam a seat. "Whisky? Rum? Tea?" he asked.

"Whisky, I think," Adam said, settling into one of the comfortable chairs.

He waited until Bill had poured them both a drink and taken his own seat before recounting that morning's discoveries.

Bill listened intently, his brows furrowed in thought. "I see."

Adam watched as he ran a hand over his chin. He seemed to be as troubled as he was.

"I can understand how you feel," Bill replied, his voice filled with empathy. "However, before jumping to conclusions, it might be best to approach Cat directly. Let her explain why she has a pistol and breeches."

Adam nodded. "You don't seem shocked."

For a moment, he thought Bill looked guarded but then dismissed it, thinking he was imagining it.

"I'm not shocked as such." Bill continued, "People keep all sorts of secrets. But it would be best to talk to her about it."

Adam stood up and walked over to the window, looking out across the manicured lawns. "You're right. I was thinking of taking the carriage down to Cornwall to visit with her and Elizabeth. I'm not certain I can wait until she returns."

"Oh, no. You don't want to do that, Adam."

Adam turned around and looked at him, immediately having the same feeling again that he was hiding something. Just as he was about to say something, there was a commotion outside the door.

A second later, Bess rushed in. She didn't even see Adam standing there and just threw herself into Bill's arms as he stood up.

"Bess! What is it? What's happened?" Bill asked.

"Cat's been taken! We came across a merchant ship, *the Malvernian,* and they attacked us before we could attack them, Bill! One of the sailors managed to overpower her, and the next thing we knew, she'd been kidnapped!"

She was talking fast, her voice full of panic, and it was only when Adam spoke that she realised he was there.

"Elizabeth, what are you talking about? What's happened?" Adam asked, feeling a pit of dread starting in his stomach. "You were supposed to be with Cat in Cornwall. What do you mean she's been kidnapped?"

Bess spun around and stared at Adam like he was the devil incarnate. "What are you doing here?"

He narrowed his eyes. "No, more to the point, what are *you* doing here?"

Bill looked from one to the other, quickly coming to a decision. "Well, you were going to find out at one time or another, so it looks like it's going to have to be now. Sit down, Adam."

He walked over and steered Adam to a chair and almost forcibly made him sit in it. Picking up his glass, he refilled it with whisky and handed it to him. "You might need this."

Adam looked from his sister to Bill. "What on earth is going on?"

Bess placed her hands on her hips. "Adam, Cat and I are captains of a pirate ship called *the Blue Belle.*"

Adam looked at her askance, and Bill added, "It's true, Adam. And I'm also the captain of a pirate ship called *the Avalon.*"

Adam took a deep slug of whisky and let the fiery liquid go down his throat before saying, "I don't know what to say."

Bess walked over to him. "I know you may find it shocking, but we've been doing it for years, and apart from the usual skirmishes, everything normally goes in our favour." She closed her eyes for a moment, getting her emotions under control before continuing. "But this time, we were not so fortunate. The merchant ship we attacked had a well-disciplined and trained crew on board."

Bill walked over to her and, placing his hand on her chin, angled her face to his. "What were you thinking? Why attack a ship like that?" He demanded angrily.

Bess scowled for a moment and retorted, "We didn't know this was going to happen. By the time McGregor warned us about the crew, they were already firing across our bow."

Adam was listening to their conversation, wondering if he'd gone mad, but no, they were definitely talking about attacking ships. He took another long draught of his whisky, shaking his head, still in a state of shock.

"We had no choice but to fight, and that's when that sailor managed to overpower poor Cat." Bess continued. "Our ship was damaged, and we had no choice but to leave. The captain threatened to sink us if we didn't." Her voice broke in a sob, and Bill immediately drew her against him.

"It'll be alright. We'll get her back." He said. "I'll send word to *the Avalon* to prepare for immediate departure. How's *the Blue Belle*?"

Bess drew away from him a little, her lashes spiked with tears, and explained, "The crew has been working day and night to repair her. Thankfully, we were able to sail back here at the same time. She's as good as she'll ever be."

Adam's heart skipped a beat, fear flooding his senses. "This is unbelievable. One minute I think my wife is in Cornwall visiting a friend, and then I find out she's a pirate!"

Bess quickly went over to him and placed her hand on his shoulder, offering comfort. "We'll get her back, Adam. I swear it."

The pieces of the puzzle began to fall into place, and Adam realised that the pistols and breeches he'd found earlier now made complete sense, as did Bill's hesitant response to his questions and even Cat's scar on her arm.

"We need to act swiftly." Bill stated, "I won't rest until Cat is safely back home."

Adam looked at Bill, his eyes filled with determination. "I'm coming with you, and don't even think about stopping me!"

"I had no intention of stopping you!" Bill shot him a wry smile. "I would do exactly the same thing if I were in your position."

The time for accusations and interrogations wasn't now, and as all three of them were united in their goal to rescue Cat, they settled down to make a plan.

Within the hour, both pirate ships were heading out of the sheltered cove and into the channel. The sea was choppy, and Adam frowned as he looked at the horizon. There was an inky blackness that he didn't like the look of.

"Are we heading into a storm?" he asked Bess.

She took out her spyglass and, squinting one eye, took a look before lowering it. "No. It's just a squall. It might be a bit bumpy, but nothing *the Blue Belle* can't handle!" She smiled at him.

He still couldn't take everything in. Seeing her dressed in breeches and wearing her tricorn hat was quite unsettling. But she was also very confident, and this was a whole other side to the sister he knew.

In fact, in a way, it was quite admirable.

Their ship was closely behind Bill's as the two ships set out on their quest to find his wife. His hands gripped the railing tightly, hoping she was unharmed. What if the merchant captain had taken advantage of her? What if he had wounded her or, worse yet, taken her life?

He closed his eyes, feeling such a sense of anger and despair that if the merchant captain came before him now, he would tear him limb from limb.

Willing his emotions under control, he felt a little hand entwine with his. It was Bess.

"Don't worry, Adam. We'll find her. We have a fair idea of where the ship will be. *The Malvernian* will rue the day they took her!"

He squeezed her hand. "I hope so. I couldn't bear life without her."

"Me neither."

The Malvernian

Cat sat across from the captain, watching as he tucked into a sumptuous meal of roast chicken and vegetables. The smell wafted over, making her salivate, but she wouldn't give him the satisfaction of knowing.

She had been on board *the Malvernian* for nearly two weeks now, and she had grown to hate the great, fat, bearded Captain Thorpe with a passion. All they had given her to eat was stale bread, the occasional piece of beef jerky, and some water. It was enough to keep her alive, but that was all.

Her eyes spat fire at him, watching as he licked the fat from his pudgy fingers and threw the chicken bone back onto his plate. How she would love to leap up and wipe that smile off his face, but a massive hand on her shoulder, belonging to a sailor called Kristos, was keeping her in place.

"So, Captain," Captain Thorpe began, "we should arrive in Portsmouth soon, and I shall take great satisfaction in handing you over to the customs men." He leaned back in his chair, patting his rotund stomach. "I must say I still cannot believe my luck that I've caught one of the notorious female captains off *the Blue Belle*. What a thorn you have been in everyone's side! But no more, my dear, no more."

Cat's heart pounded in her chest. The thought of the customs men getting hold of her was too much to bear. It was obvious Captain Thorpe relished the idea of the reward that would come his way by betraying a notorious pirate captain. Bastard.

He stood up and walked around her, his eyes glinting with malice. "We have one more stop to make before arriving in Portsmouth, so enjoy the rest of the journey. I do hope you're enjoying the comfort I have provided."

"About as much as I hope you enjoy this!" Cat kicked her leg up and, with a well-aimed strike, got him straight between the legs. His face contorted with pain, and he collapsed forward onto the floor. He could hardly breathe, let alone speak.

Kristos immediately went to his aid, and Cat, wasting no time, quickly sped for the door, but Kristos, realising she was worth too much, soon had his hands around her waist, and she was brought to a screaming halt.

"Oh, no, you don't!" He growled.

She twisted and fought, but it was of no use. Kristos was enormous, and she soon had to give up. Panting with the exertion but still defiant, she looked down at Captain Thorpe. His eyes were like marbles, and the clear anger emanating from him was truly frightening.

"Give her five lashes!" He said, his voice strained from the pain.

"Five, Captain? But she's a woman," Kristos exclaimed.

"I don't care! She plays in a man's world, so she can receive what any other pirate captain would get!" He spat angrily, his face twisted with rage.

"As you wish, Captain."

Cat struggled again. Five lashes! She couldn't take that. "Let me go!" She shrieked. "You can't do this!"

"Quit struggling!" Kristos growled at her, shoving her out of the door and up the steps to the deck.

Cat felt true terror. She had to escape. She eyed the sea, thinking about breaking free and jumping overboard, but one look at the foaming depths made her dismiss the idea immediately. To her trained eye, she could see there was a storm brewing, and raising her gaze to the horizon, she could see the inky-black clouds forming a thin, menacing line.

Looking up at the billowing sails, she gauged the wind and realised the storm was heading straight for them, and quickly too.

Kristos manhandled her over to a corner below the quarterdeck and swiftly raised both her arms, tying her wrists to some hanging ropes put there for the sole purpose of punishing disobedient crew members.

"You'll regret this!" Cat hissed.

"Brave words coming from a lowly pirate captain!" Kristos laughed in her ear.

Suddenly, the sound of thunder rumbled ominously overhead, and the sky darkened, casting a foreboding shadow over the sea.

Cat shivered and looked to the side of the ship, her eyes widening at what she saw. It was in that moment of vulnerability that help arrived, in the form of two familiar ships: *the Avalon* and *the Blue Belle*.

"Ship ahoy!" shouted a panicked voice from the crow's nest. Within seconds, *the Malvernian* was in chaos. Not only was the storm upon them, but also two fearsome pirate ships.

Cat gave a wicked smile as the raindrops began to spatter down on her, the adrenaline pumping through her at the thought of battle. Now let's see how the odious Captain Thorpe could cope with two pirate ships!

Chapter Nine

The two pirate vessels closed in on *the Malvernian,* their cannons aimed and ready. The rain lashed down and visibility was poor, but even so, Adam caught sight of his wife. She was tied up to the side of the deck, but when their eyes locked, he could see the strength within them, and it heartened him.

Bess thrust a cutlass into his hands. "Use this if need be."

The tension in the air was palpable, and Adam felt more determination than fear. If he couldn't get Cat back, then he may as well die in the process. Life without her wouldn't be worth living.

He tested the cutlass. He had fenced before and was pretty damn good, but he'd never used a cutlass before in his life. It felt heavier than a thin fencing sword, but it gave him a feeling of power. If anyone came at him, he wouldn't hesitate to use it.

He heard McGregor shouting orders to the crew, his voice cutting through the roaring wind.

"Prepare to fire!" He bellowed, his voice carrying the weight of their mission. "We have a captain to rescue, lads!"

The pirate ships manoeuvred swiftly, encircling *the Malvernian* like vengeful spirits of the sea. *The Avalon,* led by Bill, unleashed the first volley of cannon fire, the deafening roar reverberating across the waves. Explosions erupted around *the Malvernian,* sending plumes of smoke billowing into the sky.

The Malvernian's cannons retaliated, their thunderous blasts sending shockwaves through the water. The pirate ships manoeuvred skilfully, evading the onslaught of cannon fire, their crews displaying unwavering loyalty and courage.

Suddenly, Adam heard Bill's voice as he shouted across the divide to the merchant captain. "Surrender or take the consequences!"

But the merchant captain, much to Bill's annoyance, didn't acknowledge him, so the battle raged on. The pirate ships closed in on *the Malvernian*, pressing their advantage. Cannonballs tore through the air, striking the hull of *the Malvernian* with devastating force. Wooden splinters flew, masts groaned, and the cries of wounded men echoed across the sea.

Adam had never experienced anything like it, and although he found it terrifying, it was also exhilarating. The only true fear he felt was for his beloved Cat. He just hoped she wasn't harmed during the skirmish, but they had no other choice than to fight, as it seemed the merchant captain wasn't going to surrender easily.

Finally, after several more volleys, the merchant captain raised the white flag of surrender, an acknowledgement of his defeat, and soon his deck was overrun with crew from both ships.

With the surrender of *the Malvernian*, a wave of relief washed over Adam. He ran over to the railing and scanned the deck quickly to see if Cat was safe. To his immense relief, she was still standing strong, her arms tied to the ropes, but she appeared to be fine.

Victory had been achieved, and he could now take his wife home, where she belonged.

Bess came to join him and told him to remain on deck, as Bill would bring Cat back to them. As frustrating as it was for Adam to wait, he knew that he didn't possess Bill's skills, and swinging across to the other ship on a rope wasn't something he could do, let alone carry his wife at the same time!

His hair was plastered to his head from the rain, and as weary as he was, he also felt triumphant. They had won, and that was all that mattered.

Cat had never been so relieved to see a familiar face, and when Bill cut the rope from her wrists, she fell into his arms, sobbing.

Being tied up whilst the ship was being attacked had been an awful experience. Usually she would be at the forefront, her cutlass in her right hand and her pistol concealed in her jacket. But tonight, she had been rendered incapable of anything but listening to the terrible onslaught.

Bill hugged her to his muscular body. "Don't cry, Cat. You're safe now."

He quickly took her to the railing, grabbed a rope, and swung her onto the deck of *the Blue Belle*, where she was safely delivered into the arms of her husband. She was too exhausted to ask Adam why he was there and simply allowed him to lead her into the cabin, where, after shrugging off his greatcoat, he sat down in a chair and cuddled her on his lap, giving her time to recover.

She cried softly into his chest, inhaling his intoxicating male scent that she loved so much. To think that she might never have been able to do this again.

A little while later, he pulled her back a little so he could look into her face. "Let's get you out of these wet clothes. Look at you; you're drenched."

She didn't argue as he drew off her sodden clothes and wrapped her in a blanket from the bed before settling her back on his lap as he took a seat on the chair again.

"Cat, what am I going to do with you?" He said softly.

"I'm sorry, Adam. I should have told you from the very beginning."

"Yes, you should have, and for that fact alone, I'm going to punish you."

Her eyes widened. "What do you mean?"

"As soon as we return home, that bottom of yours is going to get a good roasting. That's what I mean."

"But you can't do that!" Cat breathed. "After what I've just been through."

"That's exactly why you're going to get punished. You shouldn't have even been in that position."

"But...!"

"No, Cat. There is no discussion. When we return home, you will be punished."

She looked into his eyes and knew he was resolute. She thought about protesting further but decided not to push things for now. She was just thankful to be back on her own ship and in the arms of the man she loved. Even if he did want to roast her backside.

A knock came on the door, and Cat called out, "Come."

It was Bess, with Bill right behind her.

Cat's face lit up, and she received Bess's warm embrace as she ran over to hug her. "Oh, Bess, it's so lovely to see you. I thought I wouldn't see any of you ever again!"

"Did they hurt you, Cat?" Bess said, pulling away and looking at her.

"No. It was close, though. I was due to receive five lashes, but then you arrived. I have never been more relieved."

"Five lashes?" Bill exclaimed. "What did the arrogant captain want to do that for?"

Cat gave a small smile. "Well, I managed to kick him straight in his crown jewels. He wasn't too happy."

Bill threw his head back and laughed. "Oh, how I would have liked to see his face!"

Bess squeezed her hand. "Even in the midst of such danger, you still had the gumption to hurt him! Bravo, dear Cat." She stepped back and placed her hand in Bill's. "I'm going to stay with Bill tonight on *the Avalon*, so you two can have some privacy."

"Thank you, Bess. That means a lot." Cat said happily.

"Jonas is under strict instructions to boil plenty of water so you can have a bath, and he is also, at this very moment, telling Declan what food to cook for you tonight. You must be starving for some nice food."

Cat nodded. "I've been eating beef jerky and dry bread for nearly two weeks."

"Oh, Lord!" Bess said. "Well, we'll leave you in my brother's safe hands and see you tomorrow. Rest well, dearest Cat."

The Avalon

After helping the crew empty the holds from *the Malvernian* and transfer the booty onto *the Avalon*, Bess was feeling quite weary.

Potter had served her and Bill a nice meal, accompanied by a lovely claret pilfered from right under *the Malvernian* captain's nose. So now, Bess had a lovely glow about her and was looking forward to spending the night with her massive husband. Dabbing a little perfume behind her ears, she changed into her nightgown, and looking in the little mirror in the closet, she ran the hairbrush over her dark mane, making sure she looked presentable. Considering what they'd been through, she didn't look too bad.

Walking over to Bill's large bed, she jumped on it and shot him a wicked smile. "Why, Bill, what an enormous bed you have!"

"All the better for spanking naughty bottoms on!" He said, taking a seat on the edge.

Bess's senses were immediately on high alert. "What do you mean by that?"

"Do you remember recently when my sherry barrel was destroyed?" he said, his eyes dark and brooding.

"Umm...no...I don't recall." Her face flushed beet red, and she squirmed uncomfortably.

"I didn't think you would. Well, let me refresh your memory."

She squealed as he reached for her and drew her face down across his lap. He raised her nightgown and laid his hand on her peachy little bottom, idly stroking the soft skin.

"Well, I found out the other day that someone had seen you shoot a hole in it!"

"It wasn't me!" She said hastily. "Whatever you heard, they're lying!"

"No, my sweet Bess, I think it's you that is lying."

He ran his hand down to her thighs and back up again. "So if you want a lesser punishment, I suggest you confess your sins now."

Bess pouted. "I can't get away with anything where you're concerned, can I?"

He gave a hearty laugh. "No, my sweet Bess, but it never stops you from trying, does it?"

The cabin was soon filled with her shrieks as Bill meted out a round of discipline on her naughty bottom.

The Blue Belle

Cat lay beside Adam on her small bed. He was naked, as was she, and they were entwined together tightly, neither wanting the other to ever leave their side.

A nice hot bath had been prepared for her, and Adam had bathed her gently, removing the grime from her last two weeks on the merchant ship. It was soothing, not only physically but also mentally.

After that, they had dined on some lovely food made by the ship's cook, and along with a glass of warming wine, Cat now felt sleepy and content.

She looked at her husband's face. The worry and concern for her was evident in his eyes as he returned her gaze, and his voice filled with a mix of emotions, he said. "I still can't believe that you're a pirate."

She reached out and took his hand, her fingers intertwining with his. "I'm truly sorry you had to find out this way, Adam. I only kept this part of my life secret to protect you, but it backfired, didn't it?"

"Oh, indeed it did." He said, his lips thinning with anger and disappointment.

She looked down guiltily. "I never wanted you to know. I would have told you one day. Just when the time was right."

"And when would that have been, Cat? What if that captain had taken your life? What if he had taken you against your will in bed?"

She gulped, and her lower lip trembled. "I'm sorry, Adam."

He closed his eyes for a moment, battling his temper, before looking at her once again. "I'm sorry, too, Cat. I understand you meant well, but I can't bear the thought of losing you."

A tear slipped down her cheek. "I thought I'd never see you again."

"I am here. I will always be here." He said, grazing his lips over hers. "Now, my beautiful Cat, we will discuss this more tomorrow, but for now, you need to get some sleep."

He turned her around and pulled her against his powerful body, giving her the heat and comfort she had missed the past few weeks. Safe in the arms of her husband, she soon fell asleep.

Chapter Ten

The next day

Cat awoke to kisses bestowed upon her full lips. She immediately remembered where she was, and her eyes flew open. Adam was staring down at her, his eyes caring and full of love. She stretched her arms above her head and grinned at him.

"Good morning, husband." Her eyes sparkled with desire, and she felt his hard shaft against her thigh. Reaching down, she took hold of it, her small hand wrapping around the thick length.

He closed his eyes for a moment and then said, "If you carry on, I won't be able to do what I had planned."

"And what was that husband?" She giggled, stroking her hand up and down.

He growled and quickly snatched her hand away, placing both her hands above her head and holding them tight so she couldn't move. And then, his eyes dark, he captured her lips in a fierce kiss.

She responded fervently, and when his hand dipped between her thighs, she parted them, eager to feel his touch. A touch she'd thought she would never experience again.

She was wet and ready for him, her desire burning and almost frantic. Lifting her hips, he guided himself to her entrance and slipped into her welcoming warmth.

Cat sighed with desire and arched her back, loving the full feeling as he penetrated her very depths.

"Oh, Adam!"

"My wild, sexy Cat." He said, his voice thick with emotion as he began thrusting into her, each stroke bringing them both the pleasure they craved.

Before long, she felt her body begin to soar, and raising her legs, she wrapped them around his waist, urging him deeper and deeper until, with a small cry, she climaxed. Her whole body vibrated with unadulterated pleasure. A few moments later, she felt Adam's body tighten as he gave in to his own release.

He buried his face in her neck and then fell sideways, bringing her with him, so they were facing each other.

"We are so good together, Cat. To think that I almost lost you."

She placed a finger over his lips. "Hush, my love. It is over now."

He shook his head and, raising his hand, brushed a strand of hair off her face. "Is it, though?" His gaze turned intense, and he said, "I want you to give up your life as a pirate. You don't need to do it. We have plenty of money."

Cat's gaze softened, but her determination was resolute. She had known he would ask her this question. "Adam, it's not about the money. My heart belongs to the sea and to the freedom and adventure that comes with it. But I don't want to lose you either. That's why I propose something different."

She sat up, and turning her head to look down at him, she said, "I haven't spoken with Bess yet, but I think that she should join Bill on *the Avalon*, and you should join me on *the Blue Belle*."

Adam's eyes widened in surprise, and he sat up. "You want us to become pirates together?"

A smile played on Cat's lips as she nodded. "Yes, Adam. I want us to sail the seas together."

"But I'm a lawyer!"

Cat shrugged. "So? Do both. That way, your father won't be suspicious. When you leave the practice for lengthy periods of time, you can just give him an excuse of some sort."

Adam looked at her, frowning. "I don't know if I like that idea. I don't know anything about this life. And I don't know that I want to know!"

Cat watched him carefully, and she saw a glimmer of excitement enter his eyes. "It's exciting, Adam. You already know how to use a sword, and anything else you can learn as we sail."

He lay back down on the bed and looked up at the rafters. "Could I live a life like this?" He said aloud.

Cat's eyes roved over his large, muscular chest appreciatively. "Well, I would love it. I get to spend more time with you. Which means more of this."

She moved swiftly, so she was sitting on top of him, her womanly heat covering his masculine length.

Her eyes twinkled with devilment as she moved her hips a little, and his shaft immediately hardened.

"You drive a hard bargain, wife!" He growled. "But I like it."

She soon found herself impaled, and she gasped, throwing her head back with desire. "You see, husband, this is meant to be!"

She felt his large hands on her breasts, tweaking her nipples to heated points. "I need time to think upon it, but for now, my winsome little pirate, you need taming."

Cat had no argument with that and lost all train of thought as he began to give her pleasure once more.

Later that morning

Adam stood at the railing and looked out across the vast ocean. The sun sparkled off the calm sea, creating an illusion of peace, but he knew it could change at any moment. Much like his life.

He ran a hand over his chin, feeling the beginnings of stubble. Could he live like this? Could he actually lead the life of a pirate?

He sighed, his mind in a quandary. Suddenly, a large hand slapped him on the shoulder. It was Bill.

"How are things this morning, Adam? Have you managed to clear the air with Cat?"

"Yes and no." He rubbed his brow. "Come into the cabin, and we can talk together."

Bess was already inside, laughing with Cat. They both looked every bit at ease, dressed in their men's breeches, but for him, it was still a lot to take in.

"So," Bess began, "Cat's just told me what our future plans might be, but that all depends on you, Adam."

Bill narrowed his eyes. "And what plans might these be? Am I privy to them?"

Bess sniggered. "I suppose so." She walked up to him and pointed her finger in his chest. "Cat thinks she and Adam should captain *the Blue Belle* and that I should join you on *the Avalon*. What do you say to that, Bill?"

He grabbed her finger. "For a start, my sweet Bess, don't even think about trying to boss me about!" He pulled her against him and looked deep into her eyes. "But the idea of having you on board is something I too have been thinking about."

"Have you?" Bess breathed.

He nodded. "What happened to Cat could easily have happened to you. You're mine, Bess, and I want you safely by my side."

Adam looked at them. "Why don't you give up piracy altogether?"

Bill's eyes shot to his. "I'm not ready. The time may come, but it's not now. What do you want to do, Adam?"

Adam stared back at him. There was something about being on board a ship that appealed to him. A sense of adventure that he didn't get on land. But there was also danger.

"I never thought I'd say this, but I'm willing to give it a try. If it means being with my wife and keeping her safe, then that in itself is appealing."

A sense of relief washed over Cat as she heard what Adam said. Rushing over, she placed her hands on his chest. "Do you mean it?"

He wrapped his large arms around her and drew her against him. "Yes, I do, although I can hardly believe I'm saying the words."

"You won't regret it."

Bill looked over at him and said, "I can help with sword practice, as can any of the lads. I've fenced with you, so I know you have the skills; they just need honing a little."

"I'll look forward to that." Adam said, with a smile.

"Do you want to have a go now? There's no time like the present!" Bill grinned enthusiastically.

Adam raised an eyebrow. "Why not?"

A little while later, Bess and Cat leaned with their backs against the railings and watched their husbands sword fight. Both men looked quite formidable, and it made Cat realise how Adam would fit right in. He had not only the strength of body but also of character. And a massive bonus of having him on board was that they could make love whenever they wanted!

Bess nudged her. "You look like the cat that stole all the cream!" She grinned.

"Oh, it feels so much better not to have any secrets between us." She said, still eyeing her husband. "I know how you and Bill feel now."

"You can still have little secrets, although even those can cause problems."

Cat glanced at her sharply, and noting the look in her eyes, she giggled. "Don't tell me—Bill found out about the sherry barrel."

Bess pulled a disgruntled face. "He doesn't miss a trick!"

Just as Cat began to feel a sense of peace settle within her, McGregor approached with a knowing look in his eyes.

"You see, Cat, I was right when I said you should never have secrets from your husband."

"Alright, McGregor! Enough of the 'I told you so' routine. I've learned that lesson and don't need a lecture from you." She huffed indignantly.

McGregor's weathered face broke into a warm smile. "That's the spirit, Cat. I was just looking to see if you were alright after your ordeal, and I can see that you are. Welcome back onboard, lass."

"You old goat!" She reprimanded him jovially. "I should have known. But thank you. I'm glad to be here."

He walked away, and a thought occurred to Cat. Turning to Bess, she asked, "Did *the Malvernian* have any liquor on board?"

Bess nodded. "A surprising amount, really. We've split the lot between both ships—a fair share for all."

"Excellent. I'm going to give some to Mr Clark at the tavern. He'll be so pleased."

A smile tugged at the corners of Cat's lips as she imagined the delight on Mr Clark's face when she presented him with the unexpected bounty. It was a small gesture, but one that carried immense gratitude and appreciation for his unwavering friendship.

Adam and Bill continued sparring, each enjoying it as much as the other. Bess grinned. "They do look quite magnificent, don't they, Cat?"

Cat nodded. "What a turn of events! Now, shall we have dinner together on my ship or yours, my pirate friend?"

"Oh, yours, most definitely! Let's go and tell Declan." They linked arms and descended below decks, leaving the two men enjoying their own camaraderie.

Soon the ships would be sailing for home, and Cat wanted to make the most of what might be their last time together on *the Blue Belle*.

She knew there would be challenges, but with Adam and her loyal crew by her side, she was ready to face whatever came her way.

Two weeks later, Woodleigh Manor

Cat and Adam arrived back home with a newfound appreciation of one another. They were closer now than ever.

Lord Fitzroy greeted them warmly, asking how her trip to Cornwall had gone. Cat darted a brief glance at Adam before weaving a whole story about her friend Abigail and what a marvellous time they'd all had.

She could see Adam's lips twitching as he listened to her spin her tale. It was only when they were alone later that he said, "I can see now why I was duped. Even though something felt wrong before, you are very clever at spinning a yarn."

"Is that a good thing or a bad thing?" She queried, smiling impishly.

He grabbed her to him. "I'm not sure. Although I do know that I'll have to watch you closer than ever now. Speaking of which..."

Cat raised her eyebrows, wondering what he wanted to say.

He manoeuvred her over to the bed, and her heart began to flutter with excitement, but that soon changed when he said, "I think it's high time you received your punishment."

Cat gasped and tried to pull away. "Punishment? What for?"

His eyes darkened. "Oh, don't say you've forgotten, Cat? Let me enlighten you."

The bed dipped as he sat down, and she soon found herself face down over his lap, looking at the floor.

"Now, do you remember?"

Cat thinned her lips. "You're being unreasonable."

"I thought you'd remember. And no, Cat, I'm not being unreasonable. You put your life in danger, and not only that, but you also lied to me."

"I didn't exactly lie... I just didn't tell the truth."

"A clear example of how you spin a yarn in your favour. But not today, my little wild Cat. Today, you get to experience what it feels like to tell lies to your husband."

"But Adam!" Her protests fell on deaf ears and before long, the air was filled with the sound of a wife's cries as her husband showed her the error of her ways.

Not long after, the cries turned to gasps as they made up. Their marriage even stronger than ever and their new life on the high seas waiting for their next adventure.

The end

Also by Maryse Dawson

Pirates Quest
Tides of Desire (Pirates Quest Book 1)
The Pirates Quest Collection
Captive to the Heart

Standalone
Taming the Willful Miss Roberts
Between Duty and Desire
Scandal in Silk: A Victorian Love Affair
Lily's Christmas Promise
A Passion for Annie
One Dreamy Knight

About the Author

Maryse Dawson was born in England but now lives in western France with her family - a husband, three children and two cats. When she's not writing she spends her time visiting the beaches and surrounding countryside. She has always enjoyed reading romances and loves history so began writing a few years ago to include domestic discipline in her stories. An alpha male - a feisty woman and adventures that will keep you turning the pages!

Read more at https://www.facebook.com/maryse.dawson.5.